Prince of the City: Re
By Mackenzie

For Brian, Phil and Paddy and the many cherished memories. May the hinges of our friendship never grow rusty.

"But as the years passed, he missed her more, not less, and his need for her became a cut that would not scar over, would not stop leaking."

— **Dennis Lehane, Shutter Island**

Also by the same author

The Shifting
The Book of Souls
Lost Boys
Annie's War
Ten Little Thrills
Prince of the City – The Cat's Whiskers #1
Prince of the City – Nine Lives #2
Prince of the City – Picture Purrfect #3

Recap from The Cat's Whiskers, Nine Lives and Picture Purrfect (Books 1, 2 and 3)

Vic is hired to track down whoever was holding a Persian blue cat for ransom but it was the cat's collar, or rather the charms attached to it, his employer wanted along with various factions within the city. He later learns that the discovery of charms from the illusive cat's collar, known as the *Nine Lives,* are of national importance.

He continues to work cases, while on the trail of the *Nine Lives* and under the guidance of his associate Wilf, who has contacts that go all the way up to Churchill. They hope to find out why the charms are so valuable, while fighting to keep them out of enemy hands.

Vic also wonders whether the deaths of the young men found in the river have any connection to the contents of the cat's collar, and who the mysterious female voice calling him with clues belongs to.

Vic now holds four pieces from the *Nine Lives* collection, and it seems that everyone in the city is on the trail of the five remaining items……

Book 4

Return of the Feline

Prologue

My great grandfather was captured by white slave traders in June of 1807. He was betrayed by a neighbouring Chieftain who coveted his lands and wanted his wives for himself. He watched as my great-grandfather's cattle grew fat, his two wives brought water from his well and how his people were happy and proud. After the Judas collected his money for leading all of my grandfather's able-bodied men into a trap, he had no opposition in taking what he now believed belonged to him.

The slave trade had been under attack from the abolitionists for years in England. In the year my relative was enslaved, the practice had been finally banned and when one eyed Manx Captain Hugh Crowe sailed *The Kitty's Amelia* into the port of Liverpool in October of 1807, with only six remaining slaves he was intending to sell onto rich merchants, my great-grandfather, the Crown Prince of his people, was forcibly set free.

Aboard ship conditions were appalling, and the smell of death and excrement replaced the comforting smells of his young life. He longed for the smell of lemongrass on the wind and a bowl of warm goats' milk. Instead they were fed scraps, barely sustenance, and he watched helpless as his once proud and strong men grew ill and died. But he was strong, and sheer will power alone kept him alive.

When he stumbled onto dry land, a stone underweight, hungry and cold, he was asked his name. He'd learned the English word for his once esteemed position and, thinking it would set him apart from other men, he told them his name was Prince. His genuine name was in fact Saah, meaning first boy in his home country that is now known as Liberia. The pen pushers who gave him his freedom named him Samuel Prince; I assume it was the closest they could get to Saah. He was given warm clothing and ten shillings, and set free in a world of mayhem and utter complexity, compared to a life he loved back in his country of birth. He hardly knew a word of English, but his spirit and resolve was strong; the thought of returning home as a rich man spurred him on, and he set about finding work….

So that's how I come by my unusual surname, and as a third generation Englishman and Liverpudlian, I claim the city as my own. My name is Vic Prince and I call myself Prince of the City.

Autumn 1940

1

I met Aggie at one of the big places on Upper Parliament Street. All had at least three stories and a basement. The grand edifices were built and owned by rich merchants, back when the city was the country's main gateway to trade from the Atlantic. Some had been split into apartments; others now operated as boarding houses, and this was one such place.

Air raids had continued to intensify throughout the year and on the day Italy invaded Egypt, I made my way across from where I lived on foot, mindful of the location of the public shelters along the way. We were losing the war, it was obvious to anyone but the most blindly patriotic. The Blitz of London had begun and nobody in Liverpool was under any illusion that we were in for it next, as the undisputed second city of the realm.

I reached the house without being rumbled by any of the ARP wardens who were responsible for guiding people out of the streets after dark. My black face and fleetness of foot clearly helped me avoid discovery.

I nimbly climbed the short steps up to the dark entrance and, to my surprise, an equally black face opened the huge door just as I was about to reach for the brass knocker. The woman was rail thin and buttoned up into her dark winter coat and headscarf.

"You must be Mr Prince?"

I nodded and removed my hat.

"Well don't just stand there, my niece is waiting for you in the back parlour," she said, and I stepped over the threshold. She popped her head out into the street and looked left and right. “Any sign of the warden?”

“No, Mrs Hill.”

She turned and smiled at my assumption.

“I’m Alice Grant. Agatha and I share blood but no longer a name. Anyway, I’m off to sit with her crotchety old father and listen to the wireless, assuming that nosey warden doesn’t catch up with me on the way. It was nice to meet you.”

With that she took one last look and bounded down the steps and off into the darkness, taking long loping strides until she was swallowed up by the misty September evening.

I stood in the hall for a moment remembering who it was I was meeting. Agatha Hill had been the love of my best friend Percy’s life, before the war. When she announced she was leaving him in the summer of ’38, Jimmy and I were left to pick up the pieces. They’d been together for over two years, and I mean together day and night. So, it was no surprise to me that he was drunk for four months straight from the day she walked out on him, until one autumn morning, when he dragged himself out of bed with the intention of putting it all behind him. He didn’t touch a drop of alcohol for a whole year after that, mostly to prove to himself how strong willed he was. Jimmy and I already knew he was as tough as old boots and from that day to this, her name had never been mentioned. I thought he was over her until I discovered a private shrine to Aggie in his home earlier in the year. We still hadn’t discussed it, but I hesitated, wondering how he’d react if he knew I was meeting her without even mentioning it to him. Would he consider it a betrayal?

"You going to wait in the hall all night, Victor?" Aggie called out.

"I wasn't planning on it." I followed the sound of her voice down a dark, narrow hallway, my footsteps tapping on the fine parquet flooring that had no doubt been scrubbed and polished by Aunt Alice.

I turned right, into a room where a roaring fire was lit. On either side of a fine marble fireplace stood two winged back armchairs and a low coffee table. The only light came from the flames. As Aggie rose from one of the chairs and moved to greet me, she still had that cat-like grace of movement that Percy had loved so much, and for that reason he always referred to her as the feline. She was five eight in her stockinged feet, and shapely. In fact, I thought she looked half a stone lighter than when we last met, and it suited her. She wore an A-line skirt in dark grey, beneath a plain white blouse, and the firelight danced in her dark eyes as she kissed my cheek. Her skin smelled of lemons with a hint of lavender.

I smiled down at her and she smiled back, clearly unsure how I might react.

"Let me look at you, girl. Are you eating regularly? You're skin and bone."

She laughed and raised her eyes to the ceiling.

"I wish, Vic. I lost a few pounds we both know I could afford to shed. Come on, sit down, what can I get you to drink?"

I sat and looked over at a drinks tray on the sideboard; although the light was poor, it seemed to have a bit of everything. I wanted to say, 'your aunt is clearly a customer of Percy's,' but instead I told her I'd take a scotch, no ice. She already had something on the go. If I was right, the colourless liquid was a vodka and lime, otherwise known as a gimlet. That was always her poison back in the day.

She brought my drink over, moving with the poise and balance of a dancer. Here was a woman no red-blooded male could keep his eyes off, and if I didn't know it already, it was obvious why Percy took losing her so hard.

"You haven't changed one bit, Vic."

"It's only been a couple of years, Aggie, what did you expect?"

"I don't know. It's been quite a couple of years, that's all I mean. You still sleuthing?"

"Busier than ever. What have you been up to?"

"This and that."

"Living where?"

"Here and there."

I nodded and took a belt of the good whisky. She wasn't giving much away; 'this and that,' 'here and there.' I was getting sick of it already, so I decided to speed things up a bit.

"What can I do for you, Aggie?"

"I might be able to throw some work your way."

This surprised me but I kept my expression even. I'd wrongly assumed she wanted to see me to test the water before contacting Percy. So far though, she hadn't even mentioned his name.

"Doing what?"

"I have something of high value to sell and I might need a wing man."

I fingered the brim of my hat that was in my lap and smiled. "You want me as muscle?"

"I know you're better than that, Vic, but I can pay top dollar."

"I only accept sterling," I quipped, and she frowned, "but seriously, I don't want to sound ungrateful and I know this doesn't seem like me at all, but I don't need the cash these days."

It was her turn to lean back in her chair and smile.

"Find a pot at the end of the rainbow?"

"Something like that," I said, then wiped the smile from my face. "Look, are you worried this might be dangerous? I know already this can't be a legitimate sale of goods and why, of all places, did you come to Liverpool to make this transaction? This is one of the most dangerous cities on Earth right now."

"I have my reasons for coming home and you're right, this is far from straightforward. I was just hoping to throw a little work your way for old times' sake, but I get it, you're rolling in it and don't need my money."

It was my turn to frown.

"I was hoping this might have been about something else."

She drained her glass, put it down and fixed her eyes on mine.

"Don't you mean someone else?"

I took a deep breath and another gulp from my glass, the firelight from the cut glass sending prisms of bright colours onto the dark wall.

"If he finds out we met and I didn't mention it to him, he'll be hurt and I wouldn't want that."

"I'll be gone just as quickly as I arrived. I already have a buyer."

"But you don't know if you can trust him or her?"

"Something like that." She paused to open a rectangular silver box on the table before her, filled with cigarettes. She offered me one and I put my hand up to decline. Lighting her unfiltered smoke, she inhaled deeply and removed some loose tobacco from her tongue, before turning her eyes back to mine. "You can tell him what you want. It's a matter for your own conscience, Vic."

Her reaction surprised me. I couldn't fathom how she could be so matter of fact about a man she almost married. I felt a balloon of emotion filling my chest. I tried to think with my head; nevertheless my words betrayed my feelings.

"It tore the heart out of him when you left, Aggie. He was a mess and although Jimmy and I did our best, he's never quite been the same. Never looks at other women."

"So, I've ruined him, is that what you're saying?"

"I didn't say that, but you haven't even spoken his name. The old Aggie felt things, what the hell happened to you?"

She squirmed in the chair, uncrossed then re-crossed her long legs, took a few puffs from her ciggy, then glowered at me.

"I learned a few life lessons."

"Such as?"

"That life is hard, and if you want something you have to take it, nobody is going to drop it in your lap."

My response was a hard, dry laugh, but my expression didn't alter.

"Do you think the rest of us don't already know that? Our kind get the shitty end of the stick, Aggie, and sometimes having somebody to love and hold is the only way through it. It seems to me you've got it all backwards. People are dying like flies all over Europe but instead of putting up the barriers, those of us still walking around are taking any morsel of pleasure we can."

"Look, I didn't invite you here so that you could give me a lesson in morality, Vic."

"Okay then, what am I doing here? Why me specifically?"

"I think I already said."

I shook my head.

"There are others who do what I do and plenty who are better enforcers. In my opinion, I'm only here so that you could find out how Percy is doing."

"Have it your way."

Before I could say another word there were two loud thumps on the front door. Momentarily she looked afraid.

"You expecting anyone?"

She shook her head.

I stood, put my hat on and peered down the dark passageway. I heard Aggie get to her feet and as I was in the doorway, she pressed her body against mine to look around me.

"What is that?" she asked in a virtual whisper.

"It sounds like a key in the lock."

We waited but whoever it was couldn't breach the mechanism. She stepped away from me and dug something out of her handbag. She moved beside me, now holding what looked like a Beretta semi-automatic pistol out in from of her, and she was now wearing her jacket. I gave her a queer look but before I could say anything, the door was kicked in. We saw a dark figure wearing a hat and a trench coat, with what looked to be a scarf pulled up over his lower face. It happened quickly but seemed to unfold in slow motion, as the man reached behind him and threw whatever he was holding in our direction. He turned and fled towards a waiting car while the object was still airborne. I pushed Aggie into the room and she fell backwards. I just avoided falling on top of her as the first explosion tore into the narrow space. I scrambled up and dragged her into the corner of the room, beyond the chair I was earlier using, as a second explosion shook the very foundations of the old house.

The chair had been blown on top of us and as I pushed it away, I was relieved to see that we both still had four limbs each and, apart from a few cuts and a mutually dishevelled appearance, we were unharmed. Then I heard the air raid sirens and saw the flames; I pulled Aggie to her feet. The bombing raid would give us a chance to explain the damage and should enable us to escape from the bombers, assuming they were still in the vicinity.

"Come on."

"What about my aunt's place?"

"Does she have any paying guests?"

"The last one left on Friday."

"Then there isn't anything to worry about, she's unharmed and they'll soon be on their way to put the fire out. Afterwards, if this place isn't up to it, I suppose she can stay with your dad. Right now, we need to get out of here while this is going off."

She nodded, straightened her clothing, put her pistol away and led me to the rear of the property and out into a smoky, rectangular yard, containing an outside toilet and a heap of coal.

Aggie peered in disgust at the six-foot wall that led to the back entry. I smiled, lacing my hands together and holding them out in front of me. She shook her head, removed her shoes, put them in her bag then hoisted up her skirt, displaying long, smooth, muscular legs. I tried hard not to look and ignore the feel and smell of her, and although I succeeded, it occurred to me that I'd never before been so intimate with Miss Agatha Hill. She might possess a heart of granite, but she was still only flesh and blood.

She dropped on the other side and I scrambled over the wall, after her.

"Do you have a piece, Vic?"

"A piece? What are you, an extra from a Jimmy Cagney movie?"

This made her smile.

"No, I don't, Aggie, you know how I hate those things."

"Then I'm glad I have this," she said, pulling the Beretta out from her bag again.

I spread my hands.

"So, this attempt on your life is not completely unexpected? What are you mixed up in, Aggie?"

"I didn't think you were interested."

"Let's just say I'm concerned enough to care whether you become just another statistic."

She smiled again; it was a smile that told me she'd got the reaction she'd been hoping for.

"Where to?" she asked.

Now it was my turn to smile. I pushed my hat back and shook my head.

"Follow me and stay close. Oh, and try not to shoot anyone along the way."

She reached down and put her shoes back on, adding a couple of inches to her height. She followed close by as we wound our way to my office, crisscrossing the city, using as many back entries as we could.

We got to Harry's garage just as the all clear was sounding. The forecourt was ink black as we approached the stairwell that led to my first-floor office.

She followed me up and I switched on a lamp, and got us both a stiff drink.

"What now?"

"Now I want to know what nearly got us both killed tonight. What exactly is it you're selling?"

"I was prepared to tell you, assuming you'd agree to help."

I smirked. "Can't a bloke change his mind?"

"Then you'll help?"

"I will, but only because Percy would have my hide if I let anything happen to you. So, what gives? What are you peddling?"

"It's better if I show you."

I raised an eyebrow. "You have it on you?"

"You'll need to turn around, Victor."

I was sat at my desk, she was across from me, so I swivelled my chair around to face the wall. I heard her stand, followed by a cracking sound I couldn't place. Then there was a jangle of metal and as she invited me to turn around, I was sure my mouth must have been open, wider than the Mersey tunnel. Before me on my desk stood four of the five remaining pieces from the *Nine Lives.* Four miniature moggies in different poses.

"Do you know what they are?"

"No idea, but they're my meal ticket, Vic. I've been offered a mouth-watering sum for them."

"I don't doubt it. They're the hottest property this side of the pond. No wonder you need protection."

I picked up the phone.

She suddenly stiffened. "Who are you calling?"

"Someone we can trust, who'll find you somewhere safe to stay."

She lit a cigarette and immediately looked like the cat who'd got the cream.

"I always knew I could count on your help, Victor."

I said nothing and dialled.

2

I was attending to a few minor cuts on Aggie's face, when I heard footsteps on the stairs moving fast. She reached for her bag and I was sure she had her finger on the trigger of her gun, as Percy waltzed in, carrying a wooden crate. I had cotton wool in one hand, iodine in the other. He was smiling when he saw me and if he was shocked at the sight of the woman seated next to me, the feline herself, the love of his life, then he handled it supremely well.

"Oh Vic, I didn't realise you had company. I just wanted to drop off a few goodies. I didn't know if you'd be up and about this early, but I thought I'd take a chance."

"You're up pretty early yourself," was all I could say as a silly, nervous grin flowered on my lower jaw. My mind was racing. I'd wanted to break this to him gently and never wanted him to find out like this.

While I was treading water, Aggie handled it beautifully. She stood and moved to where he waited with her usual grace, placing her long fingers on his cheek, and kissing him on the lips. She then pulled at his lapels and smiled sweetly at the man she'd left in bits, two years and three months ago.

"Business must be good. You look and smell like a million dollars."

"What can I say, petty crime pays," he responded, moving past her to place the crate containing booze, French cheese, and fresh vegetables on my desk. He didn't even look at me. I assumed he was using all his concentration to keep his emotions in check.

"I was up early to meet a clandestine shipment, what's your excuse?" he said to both of us, but looked at Aggie, leaning back on my desk.

"We haven't been to bed yet, Percy. I coerced Vic into helping me with something and we got into a little trouble. Oh, and before you lose it with him, I didn't want you to know I was in town, but he insisted you had to know. I'm sure mine is the last face you ever wanted to see again."

He was still smiling, and I don't think he could trust himself to answer that particular question.

"I was planning to come right over after we'd got Aggie to a safe house."

"We?"

"Wilf's offered to help and I was hoping to get Harry to drive us over there, just as soon as he gets his lazy arse out of bed."

"Why wait? My car's outside."

He pushed himself upright and walked past me, still not looking directly at me. Aggie linked him and they descended the stairs like an old married couple. I followed, a feeling of dread looming over me and an acidic feeling at the pit of my stomach; it could have been hunger but felt much more like treachery.

Out on the deserted forecourt a light drizzle was falling; in the distance the river was slate grey and choppy, helped along by a stiff dawn breeze.

Everton Cosgrove sat at the wheel of Percy's white rolls Royce, a used matchstick in his mouth. He stepped out and Percy introduced Agatha as an old friend. His dead eyes appraised her and I couldn't remember if he knew their history. They climbed in the back and I got in beside Cosgrove.

"Where to Vic?"

I explained that we needed to get to Hoylake.

"I was thinking about the ferry but for safeties sake, I was going to ask Harry to take us the long way around."

"Skirting north Wales you mean?"

Cosgrove offered me one of his rare smiles.

"We don't need to go all that way when there's a perfectly serviceable tunnel under the Mersey."

"But I thought civilians were no longer allowed through?"

"Not strictly true, Vic. Percy has special dispensation," he said, winking at me and starting up the car.

"I bet he does," I replied.

The tunnel was now only kept free for the armed forces and emergency services, but Percy was probably supplying somebody with enough contraband to waive us through. As we set off through the dreary, early morning weather, I sneaked a glance at Aggie and Percy in the wing mirror, talking and laughing together on the back seat like two best friends. It occurred to me that they were both exceptional actors. I knew my closest friend still carried a torch for the woman, and she'd done her utmost to give me the impression that she couldn't care less whether she ever saw him again. What was true? I didn't know but I didn't like it, as I squirmed in my seat all the way through the tunnel. Once we were on the Wirral, Percy instructed Cosgrove to detour to a greasy spoon that served our kind, after learning that Aggie hadn't eaten for hours. He took a route through the back streets of Birkenhead, that included a drive past Tranmere Rovers football ground.

We eventually stopped at a place called Mama June's, a hangout for sailors and merchant seamen of all race and creed.

Our car and our fancy clothes got us a few peculiar glances, but when Percy offered to buy everybody's breakfast, the half dozen or so patrons inside suddenly took less interest in who we were and how we looked. Mama June was a larger than life character in her mid-forties, of mixed race. Her coffee coloured brow was beaded with sweat, but her accent was pure Liverpudlian.

"What can I get you gents?"

We ordered three fry ups and four cups of builders' tea, while Aggie had two poached eggs on toast. I assumed because of what was on the menu, this was another of Percy's happy customers.

Percy paid up as promised and we walked out to the car, heroes of the greasy spoon brigade. Cosgrove got behind the wheel and once more took a less than straightforward route to our destination.

The safe house was the very last one on Stanley Road in Hoylake. A good location. If anyone was planning to cause mischief, they'd be seen coming for more than a mile on a long straight road. When I considered the location, I told myself the place probably had a vessel stored somewhere on the property, just in case a quick getaway was called for.

We pulled onto the deliberately noisy gravel drive and immediately our eyes went to the right of the place. We each took another look at the neighbouring property, which just happened to be a lighthouse, sporting a new coat of brilliant white paint. I was unsure whether it was still a working aid to sailors, or if it was now privately owned. To the left of the detached house before us was a sea of green grass, running down to a narrow strip of beach, looking out over the Dee estuary and Wales beyond. I was sure it must have been an absolutely stunning view during peacetime, but the barbed wire that stretched along the tidemark rather spoiled it. Aggie climbed out and whistled at the sight of the large double fronted property before her. A balding giant of a man, wearing a polar neck jumper and corduroys, stepped out of the front door right on cue and joined us on the expansive driveway. A bulge in his right pocket could only have been a firearm, so I decided not to stare. He told us he was Toby, in a voice that seemed an octave too high for a man as mean looking as he was. He shook each of our hands and said he was expecting only one guest. Percy stepped forward to do the talking and it seemed he'd already made his mind up about something.

"Is it just you here, Toby?"

"I have a man who comes in after dark."

"Would it be alright with you if Everton here, hangs around for the duration?"

By the look on Cosgrove's narrow face this hadn't been discussed.

"I'd need to clear this with Mr Henderson but if it's okay with him, I'd be more than happy to accommodate your friend."

"Can you check with him then, please?"

"Certainly, Mr Holding."

"Call me Percy, I've never been comfortable as mister anything."

He nodded and went off to call Wilf.

"You okay with this, Everton?"

"You're the boss."

"I think Wilf's the boss around here," Percy added, continuing to make a series of smiles. Anyone who didn't know what was playing out, might think he was the happiest man alive. He then looked at me properly for the first time, since he'd stumbled across Aggie in my office.

"Can I drop you anywhere, Vic?"

"No, that's okay. I'm going to get the lay of the land here and when I'm ready, I'll jump the ferry back across. Thanks, anyway."

Before he could respond, Toby reappeared.

"I've been given the green light. He says the lady is only here for a short stay."

"I am, Toby," she answered for herself.

"Shall I take you up to your room, Miss?"

"Sure," she answered, offering him a wan smile. She then planted a final kiss on Percy's cheek, only glancing at Everton and I as she followed Toby into the house. He watched her go, another wide grin backing up his award-winning performance. I couldn't look at him, I felt sick to my stomach. It seemed to me that instead of perspiration, guilt was escaping from my glands. Before leaving he said something to Everton in a low voice. Too quiet for me to hear.

"Later, Victor," was all he said as I was looking out into the brightening picture over the estuary, with my back to him. I only turned as he wheel spun off the drive and sped off in the direction we'd come from, only this time he wasn't smiling.

*

Cosgrove turned to me and asked, "Have you and Percy fallen out?"

"Why d'you ask?"

"You hardly said two words to each other."

"Let's take a walk around the grounds and have a little talk." I started up but he put the brakes on. "What is it?" I asked.

"I'd rather not if you're going to piss in my soup over what I just said."

"Piss in your what?" Now it was my turn to smile. "Come on, Everton, I just want to talk about a few things."

"I'd rather not, if this is going to be one of your sermons."

"When did you become so sensitive?"

"I have feelings too, Vic, just like everybody else."

Not when there's trouble brewing you don't, I thought, but didn't say it. Instead I held my hands up, in mock surrender.

"Come on, Everton, I promise not to pick on you."

"Talking like that is liable to get you a thick lip."

"That's more like it, come on, let's take Shanks's pony."

"Shanks's what?"

"Never mind, let's walk."

We finally moved onto the grass; it was still damp from the drizzle that had fallen earlier in the day, but the short and sculptured lawn was firm underfoot, after a particularly hot summer. We started off on the beachside, intending to swing around to the rear and do a complete circumference of the place. I did want to talk to Cosgrove but I was also interested in understanding how secure this place was, particularly in view of the cargo Agatha was carrying. Ideally, I would have stayed the night too. But on this very evening, Mei-Li had taken the night off from her job at

The White Oyster club and arranged to invite our fathers over to discuss our wedding day, that was pencilled in for Boxing Day 1940. I knew well enough that if I missed the 7pm dinner date at our one room apartment, I might as well forget about turning up on the day.

"Did Percy mention anything about who Agatha is?"

Everton thought for a moment and threw away the umpteenth match he'd chewed that morning, before answering.

"He just said it was important to him that she stayed safe. Why, who is she?"

I took a deep breath before I explained it to him. Once again, I felt uncomfortable discussing Percy's love life but I thought it better if Everton knew just how valuable Aggie was, at least in Percy's eyes. I told him everything but left out the bit about him still carrying a torch for her. In his inimitable way, all he said was,

"I see."

Everton was a man of few talents but his focus when trouble came calling was one of them, and the reason for telling him was to put him on red alert.

I also left out the bit about the four pieces from the Nine Lives collection she was carrying, but Everton was no fool.

"I get the Percy connection, but why is she hiding out at one of Wilf's safe houses?"

"I went to Wilf because I didn't want to involve Percy. I wasn't sure how he'd react if he knew I was meeting her without telling him."

"So that explains the trouble between you?"

"I suppose."

"What did she want you for?"

"She wanted to offer me a job that was more suited to your line of work. Although I didn't get the chance to delve too deep, before a bomb was chucked down the lobby of her aunt's place on Parliament Street."

"Did you see the bomber?"

"It was dark but he was white, and before you ask, I didn't get a look at the driver either."

Everton smacked his lips together as though I might have been describing his favourite food.

"Been a while since I shot myself a whitey."

"Whoa, now just hold on. If you can, you detain, not kill these good gentlemen, should they pay you a visit."

"Whatever you say, Vic."

"I mean it, Everton; we need to know who they are."

We'd reached the back of the property and I noted that, being a corner plot, the rear also ran down to open water. I supposed it was accessible by boat but if anyone tried it, they'd also had to get past the barbed wire. I liked the fact that the lawn was so big and open that any potential invasion by water would be seen. I also noted that the place had intruder lights that were activated by pressure pads. They lit up as we walked by. I'm sure that broke all of the blackout rules but then again, a lot of what Wilf did involved national security, so I don't imagine he cared about that too much. Also built into the rear of the house was a triple garage and as we sauntered past, I noted that all the doors were up. Inside, Toby was polishing a bright blue Wolsey Ten Hornet, two-seater. Beside it stood a motorboat on a trailer, to the right of which was a Land Rover. He waved to us and I smiled at the sight of the vessel. I knew right away they'd either found or made a weak spot in the barbed wire, just in case they needed a quick getaway.

Wilf wasn't running a tin pot operation.

"You took an odd route from the tunnel to the café and then from the café to here, why is that?"

"You noticed then, I thought you might."

"I'm not in the habit of traveling from Birkenhead to Hoylake via Scotland."

He either ignored my quip or didn't find it funny.

"I had a feeling we were being followed."

"A feeling?"

"I didn't see anything that gave me cause but there was something, call it a sixth sense I get when I think I'm being watched. It was probably nothing."

I didn't think it was the time to debate the rationale behind skills we can never quite explain, but I knew what he meant and have often felt something similar myself. I was rarely wrong about it.

"You did the right thing, Everton."

He looked at me as though I'd offended him.

"Is that a compliment, Vic?"

"I suppose so but don't get used to them."

He shook his head as we walked on.

*

We went inside and had a coffee with Toby, who was as adept at brewing up as he was at baking it seemed. I only hoped he was as handy as he looked if the safe house was attacked. He'd baked a carrot cake using some of his meagre rations, telling us he used carrots he grew in his garden at home. It looked and smelled good, and I decided to have a piece despite my large breakfast, on the basis I probably wouldn't have anything for lunch. It tasted great, considering Toby explained that it was made with hardly any sugar, powdered egg, and water instead of milk. Although the accompanying coffee was heavily laced with chicory, it was drinkable.

"The cake is good. Too good for females, I suppose," I said.

"I've already taken a piece up to Miss Hill."

"I see. Is she confined to her room the whole time she's with you?"

He shook his head and offered me a brief smile, then added,

"After blackout she can have the run of the place. You see, our protocols assume anyone could pick her off with a high-powered rifle and a scope, during daylight hours."

"What are you told about the people who are brought here, Toby?"

"Nothing. As far as we're concerned it's classified."

I smiled and narrowed my eyes.

"How much do you know about us?"

"I promise you, it's on a need to know basis only," he said and offered another fleeting smile, before averting his eyes in Everton's direction. "My night man is partial to a game of cards, if you play?"

"That sounds just the ticket to keep me awake."

I stood, put my hat on my head and fastened up my jacket.

"That was really nice of you. I need to get going. I have a long walk from here to the ferry terminal."

"Don't do that, Mr Prince..."

"Call me Vic and this is Everton."

He smiled. "Got it. I was going to suggest that Everton take the Wolsey and drive you over there."

"If you're sure."

"I insist," he said.

We shook hands and he handed Everton the keys, as he cleared the plates and cups.

"When you get back, Everton, I can offer you a room to sleep in for the afternoon and I'm more than happy to wake you before I'm relieved."

Everton thanked him and followed me outside.

Toby had obviously never seen Everton drive and as we headed around the back to the garage, I warned him that the two-seater handled light and that he shouldn't take the corners too fast.

"You sound more like my mother each day, Vic."

I almost said, 'I knew you didn't have a father, but you actually have a mother?' I thought better of it as I was soon to be in close quarters with Mr Cosgrove, and remembered his reaction to my crack about his sensitivity.

My comments clearly provoked a reaction from this new-found sensitive side of stone killer Everton Cosgrove, as he drove like we were in a funeral procession. On the way, I explained why I couldn't stay in Hoylake with him overnight, but as usual it was impossible to read his reaction from the limited range of expressions he projected. When we got to the ferry terminal, I shook his hand and walked over to stand with a handful of elderly citizens, to wait for the next ferry to arrive. There were rumours that they wouldn't be running the service for much longer because of the risk of sea mines in the Mersey estuary, and I thought of the issues that could cause for families, cut off from each other by a narrow strip of water.

Yet another symptom of war.

*

It was around one o'clock when I got back to Harry's Autos. I popped my head into the office, to check whether there was any mail or messages for me. Harry's secretary, Wendy, was a tall, shapely blonde, who liked to verbally joust with me whenever I set foot in her domain.

"Why, hello, handsome. If it's Harry you want, he's out collecting a customer's car. I hope you don't think because of that you can take advantage of me though."

I smiled and pushed my hat to the back of my head.

"I strongly doubt whether any man has ever gained the upper hand with you, Wendy."

She put her index finger up to her full lips and struck a pose.

"There was that one time, but it's so long ago I hardly remember it."

"Now I know you're pulling my chain."

"Ha ha, what do you really want?"

"Can't you guess?"

"Let me think, you've either come to tell me you're calling the wedding off because you can't live without me and we're eloping to Switzerland, or you want to know if I have anything for you."

I raised an eyebrow and smiled.

"Aren't you forgetting you are, in fact, a married woman?"

She flashed me a wicked smile.

"Oh, that doesn't stop people when there's a war on, Vic, those rules no longer apply."

"And if I was only after my mail and messages?"

"That's not worth mentioning because there aren't any."

"Of course not; I'll just go and book our passage on the next vessel to Switzerland."

"You can't fool me, Vic, I know that place is landlocked."

"They say that but that's just so they can make sure travel by sea stays exclusive," I quipped and headed for the door.

"See you later then, ship mate."

I shook my head, walked outside, and looked up at the darkening clouds overhead and felt the wind stiffen. It looked as though we might be in for it. I just hoped the storm abated by the time I was ready to make my way home. I unlocked the ground floor door, to my first-floor office, and launched myself up the narrow staircase. When I got inside, I brewed some of the good coffee, threw my feet on the desk and forced myself to sit in quiet contemplation before bringing my accounts up to date. It was a job I'd been putting off for weeks but, instead, thinking my way through all that had occurred in the past 24 hours, I found myself staring at the telephone and wondered whether I should call Percy and tell him Agatha was in good hands from what I could tell. I didn't like the way we'd parted back in Hoylake but I thought my reason for calling was a bit thin; after all, he'd seen the place for himself and he knew the kind of operation it was. He knew Wilf harboured VIPs, diplomats and even politicians during these difficult times, so he was certain to know that an ex-girlfriend on the make should be no problem at all.

I took off my hat and jacket, rolled up my sleeves, then proceeded to make a decent job of my financials. I stretched, yawned and was about to close up when the phone rang. I answered it after one ring, worried it might be Wilf.

It was Percy.

"I thought I'd catch you, Vic, before you left for the last supper."

"You know about tonight?"

"Your dad mentioned it to Paul."

"I see."

"Look, Vic, it was a surprise to see Aggie after all this time and it unearthed some old feelings, but I want you to know that I get why you didn't say anything."

"You do?"

"Come on, Vic, do you think I still carry a torch for her or something?"

The answer was, I knew he still did but I decided not to mention that.

"I didn't know what to think but, please understand Perc, I thought she was back in town to see you and I assumed she wanted to sound me out first."

He laughed and it sounded hollow, lacking in authenticity down the phone line.

"I'm sure you thought about calling and hesitated a few times, just like me, but let me be clear, I don't ever want Agatha Hill to come between us. The same way I know you'd never let Mei-Li interfere in our friendship."

At the sound of his words I exhaled properly for the first time that day.

"You nailed it, Percy. I was worried that you thought I'd let you down. I'm so pleased you called."

"That makes two of us, Vic, but look, there is something else you should know about Aggie."

"Go on."

"You can't trust a word she's told you."

His comments hit like a depth charge and genuinely shocked me, especially coming from his lips.

"You still there, Vic?"

"I'm listening."

"Almost everything she told me about what she's been up to and where she's been these past years is a lie."

"And you know that how?"

"It pays to have a few contacts in my game. I ask about her from time to time and I've learnt certain things."

"Then you do still have feelings for her?"

When he answered, his voice sounded thick with emotion.

"It's been hard to move on, Vic, I won't lie, but I now see her in a way I couldn't before. I was besotted with her back in the day and couldn't see her faults, but like all of us she has them. She's always been obsessed with making a big score and I think whatever she's mixed up in, she sees this as the big one. What worries me though is how she acquired whatever it is she's selling and why somebody was prepared to bomb a boarding house, that could have been teaming with guests, just to get at her."

*

I bathed and changed before our fathers arrived. We saw a lot of Mei-Li's father, Ling Chen, living under the same roof, yet occupying separate dwellings above his herb shop. By the time I was ready, he'd joined us and was dressed in clothing I'd never realised he even owned. He wore a well-cut lounge suit, in charcoal grey, and it looked good on him. Normally he'd wear the traditional dress of his people, which as my girl explained to me not long after we'd started dating, was something called a changshan, a kind of long robe, which he constantly wore in a variety of colours. It did puzzle me why he conformed to the accepted dress code of his community. Mei-Li's mother, Charlotte, was white and after they were married, he was ostracised by his family and friends; this continued long after her death during the *Spanish Flu* epidemic of 1919, so that he was never quite accepted back into their close-knit society. They still bought his herbs and listened to his advice, yet treated him appallingly in our opinion.

Mei-Li and I knew what it was like to be outcasts, and the last thing we would have done was try to please them by dressing the way they expected.

My father joined us shortly afterwards and I was pleased he was starting to gain some weight, after spending eight months in hospital. He seemed to be getting stronger and sharper every day. Even though the doctors explained that he'd seemingly recovered from some sort of mental breakdown, they couldn't guarantee his malady would never return. We'd always been close and, because I thought I was losing him some months before, I doted on his every word. I threw my big arms around him as he walked in.

"Easy, Vic, let me breathe, son."

"There's more of you to get hold of now, pop."

He smiled. "It's all this good cooking."

"Paul tells me he's tried fattening you up, but you've become a fussy eater in your old age."

He and Paul Okilo, Percy's driver and Dad's oldest friend, were living together in his two-up two-down.

He smiled. "It isn't that, Vic, I don't yet have the appetite that I used to. And I know Percy can provide for us, but there's plenty of people in this city who are living on the breadline."

"All the more reason to eat what's in front of you."

"I can see this is an argument I'm never going to win."

Mei-Li, who looked stunning in a little black number, gently manoeuvred my big frame out of the way and kissed my father on the cheek.

"Ignore him, Charles. Come and sit." She turned to me. "Vic, stop picking on our guests and pour us all a glass of wine."

I did as instructed and in our compact one bedroom flat, I marvelled at how my girl had re-arranged the furniture and set a beautiful table, after cooking a Chinese banquet fit for a king, or perhaps a Prince. Or soon to be 3 Princes, to be precise.

We ate and drank, and Mei-Li explained our wedding plans. It was to start at Brougham Terrace registry office, a place where all births and deaths within the city were certified. We were then planning to move on to the White Oyster club at Carlos' insistence.

"That's all great, Vic, but Ling Chen and I had a little talk and we would feel better about it if we could contribute."

The Chinaman put down his chopsticks and nodded vigorously.

"Dad, we're grateful, but for once in our lives money is not what we need. We just want your blessing, not your cash."

"Well, I know I also speak for Ling Chen when I say that, unless you accept our financial involvement, I'm afraid we won't feel able to attend."

I was exasperated and, seeing this, Mei-Li placed her small hand on my arm and said,

"What do you propose?"

"We both wish to contribute one third of whatever the total cost is."

"Then we accept," she said before I could answer, and I could do no more than raise my eyes to the ceiling, then smile, before shaking the hand of each man. Mei-Li stood and hugged them both.

"Where will you live when you're hitched? I assume you'll have enough from the Henry Swan money to buy a place?"

"We will and we plan to, but rather than buy a house only to see it blown to bits in an air raid, we're going to rent until this damn war is over."

Both of our fathers smiled and reached for their wine glasses.

"Well, I'll raise a glass to that," my father added and I sat back and relaxed, hoping the Jerries would leave us alone and let us enjoy what was left of our evening.

3

Paul picked me up next morning in a scarlet Riley 8 that was one of Percy's work horses. I climbed inside and shook his hand. He'd agreed to give me a lift to Wilf's main residence on the edge of the extremely select Hale village, a stone's throw from the airport and the nearby working-class community of Speke.

"How's your head, son?"

"Still attached. How's my Dad's?"

"No idea. I left him in his pit."

"Is he okay?"

"Just fine. He was rather merry, as you know, when I picked him up last night, that's all, so I let him sleep it off. Don't forget, since he's joined the world again, he's been easing himself into things slowly. What I'm trying to say is you've no need to worry. Your father is one the most astute men I've ever met, Vic; despite all he's endured this year he knows how to conduct himself, particularly when alcohol is involved."

"Are you two getting along okay?"

"Just dandy, son. We're like an old married couple. After we've eaten, we draw the blackout curtains, open a bottle of beer and listen to the wireless, until one of us falls asleep in his armchair."

"Just like old times?"

"Not even close. We were young and full of vim and vigour back then. The stories of what we got up to when we were even younger than you are now, would make a man of the cloth blush."

I chuckled but before I could utter another word, he looked in his rear-view mirror, tightened his grip on the wheel and made a sharp and unexpected left turn. Then he looked in the passenger view mirror and said,

"I knew it."

"What is it?"

"We've picked up a tail."

"Can you lose them?"

"Probably."

"I adjusted my position slightly and looked over my shoulder and saw a black Morris Oxford was following. Two blurred white faces was all I could make out, both wearing hats. It made me wonder if they were the bombers, remembering that Everton had a feeling of being watched on the way over to Hoylake.

Paul deliberately drove into a built-up area he knew and quickly said, "Hold onto your hat, this might get a little bumpy."

He looked once again into his mirror, floored the Riley, taking a sharp right and then a handbrake turn, immediately left, at a minor crossroads. Directly ahead was a couple of houses that had been hit during a bombing raid. He then floored it again and I told myself there was no way we were heading for a pair of bombed out houses. I couldn't have been more wrong. He didn't even brake and we sailed through what was, until recently, somebody's front parlour. We missed colliding with the rickety looking structure by a whisker; I banged my head on the roof twice, as we shot out the other side and back onto a far more amenable road surface. We continued on as if nothing had happened and after ten minutes of silence, and a couple of detours, Paul announced that we'd lost them.

When we eventually reached Wilf's place, we had to wait to be buzzed through and I noted that security had been upgraded since my last visit in the spring.

He drove me to the front door, where a bloke the size of a small gorilla opened the car door and patted me down, before I was let through. Paul, who'd waited to give me the thumbs up, was waved off unceremoniously by the same mean looking giant.

*

The house reeked of old money. Double doors that must have been twelve foot in height, led to an enormous entrance hallway that had genuine marble floor tiles. Wood panelling adorned the walls, and in the centre of the foyer stood a bowl of white crocus, giving off a scent reminiscent of jasmine. I was admiring the flowers when I heard footsteps to my left.

"Why, Victor, I never pegged you as a horticulturist."

I looked up and saw Ginny Merrill, Wilf's much better half. She was still trying to gain weight after being shot full of holes in the spring, when she was in the employ of John Smith, a slippery character who ran covert operations in Liverpool for the United States. She was that rare thing, incredibly feminine but as tough as teak.

"If I knew what the word meant, I might be able to discuss it."

She laughed and walked toward me, planting a big one on my cheek, reaching up on her tip toes as she did. She smelled sweeter than the crocus and whenever I was in her company, it reminded me what a lucky son of a gun Wilf was. She linked me and walked me to the open door she'd earlier come through.

"Now, come on, Victor, this is one of your English words and I know you have a better vocabulary than you like to let on. With a father who read him Keats at bedtime, no less," she said in her southern drawl.

I sniggered as we found ourselves in a narrow brightly lit corridor, that looked more modern than the rest of the place, with plain white walls and half a dozen closed doors that might actually fit an aperture in an ordinary person's home.

"I don't think Wilf showed you his little home from home operation when you were last here?"

"He didn't and I don't remember you needing muscle at the front door either."

She said nothing and disentangled herself. I followed her through another open door, into a room that was filled with hundreds of hard back books and a big oak desk, where Wilf sat, frowning at a document. He stood and smiled as I entered.

"Vic, thank you for coming. I hope you're hungry. I arranged for us to have brunch while we discuss our approach with Agatha."

He'd inclined his head to two blood red chesterfield settees, behind his desk and arranged at right angles to each other, around a rectangular table. On it were cups, a coffee pot, plates, cutlery and two metal dome-like receptacles. It smelled delicious and I was suddenly pleased I'd only had a minute piece of stale bread and butter with my morning tea.

Wilf sat beside Ginny and I faced them as he poured us each a cup of steaming hot coffee.

"I take it brunch is what you rich folks call eating between meals."

Wilf smiled again, helping himself to some scrambled egg and crispy bacon.

"Well, we won't force you to eat."

"I wouldn't want to appear rude."

I proceeded to fill my plate with double Wilf's portion and Ginny wasn't far behind me.

"Vic was wondering why you had Alec on the front gate, frisking people no less," Ginny said.

"Oh, that. Well, we've received intel that indicates all those with the ear of our cigar smoking chief are on a Third Reich hit list. Anyway, enough about my problems, tell me all about Agatha's unexpected return."

I did, leaving nothing out, and he and Ginny ate and drank while my food grew cooler. When they started to speak, I wolfed most of my own food down and slurped my coffee.

"So, it's clear that somebody wants her dead. Is that about the cargo she's holding or something else, do you think?"

Wilf had a way of getting right to the root of a situation, and it reminded me of a question that had occurred to me just after the attack at her aunt's house.

"Would someone from our side try to kill Aggie, to stop her selling part of the *Nine Lives*?"

Wilf looked pensive before answering.

"It's something we might consider if she was determined to sell to our enemies but, as far as I'm concerned, this is the first we've heard of Miss Hill and the four pieces."

"Assuming they haven't kept it from you."

"Vic, I have to admire your scepticism."

“It’s my most endearing quality, Wilf, and it goes with the territory. In my line of work, it pays to be a cynic.”

“To answer you straight, if one of our people went after Agatha without my knowledge, it could only be a splinter group who’d gone rogue. But from what you’ve told me, this has all the hallmarks of a poorly executed attempt on her life. If the people I employ were asked to take her out, it would have happened in a way to minimise a wider loss of life. They would have been patient and dealt with her, preferably during the blackout once they’d cornered her alone somewhere.”

For some reason, the thought of Aggie dying after dark, her body dumped in a stinking entry, sent a shiver down my spine and I put down my fork.

“Lost your appetite, Victor?” Ginny asked.

“Mental images of my best friend’s former fiancée, dying at the hands of an assassin, will do that.”

Wilf put down his own plate and lit up a cigarette. Ignoring my sensitivities, he put forward a theory.

“This looks to me more like something personal. I think somebody wants her dead and they don’t particularly care who they have to take down with her to do it.”

“Oh goody, we already have a boat load of enemy agents with a hard on for the *Nine Lives,* and now somebody else is possibly trying to execute some sort of blood feud.”

“Did she say she had a buyer for the pieces?” Ginny asked, offering me one her smokes. I turned it down and she lit up, inhaling deeply.

"Not in so many words, but my impression is that she was prepared to put her head above the parapet to get this deal done."

"What will convince her to hand them over to us?" Wilf asked.

"Money. According to Percy she's fantasised about making one big score her entire adult life. I bet she's already worked out what she's going to do with her take. If he's right, she's getting off on it."

"Focused and highly motivated. A dangerous combination," Ginny remarked.

"Is she packing?" Wilf asked.

"You bet."

"Can she use it?"

"Her old man treated her like the son he never had. She can shoot, fish and compete with any man at any game, even cards."

"She sounds quite the catch."

"She is, Ginny. Percy thinks he's fooling me. He still loves her but, perhaps he's being honest with himself now and is prepared to consider her many flaws."

Ginny stubbed out her cigarette, stood and stretched, then looked across at Wilf.

"I'll go and check she's ready."

As she left the room, I raised a quizzical eyebrow at Wilf.

"We're planning to cruise up there on the *Windjammer*."

"Of course we are," I said and reached for my hat.

*

We left Wilf's ten bedroomed mansion, accompanied by another member of his security team. A beanpole of a man they referred to as Jim, who could have been mute as far as I was concerned, because he never uttered a single word in my presence. We made our way to Wilf's personal quayside, via fourteen stone steps. Our position was almost at the narrowest point of the Mersey estuary, and Wilf's forty-foot motor cruiser was fired up and ready to go. Bill was at the helm, a grey haired, bearded bloke in his fifties, with a pleasant smile, but under his knitted polar neck his body was roped with muscle, and I noticed white scarring on his knuckles. Ginny attempted to pass me a handgun but I kept my hands in pockets.

"Is that compulsory now?"

She shook her head, laughed, and chucked it back into her bag.

The sun was trying to break through the cloudbank overhead and beneath them floated barrage balloons, intending to discourage enemy aircraft. A fat lot of good they were doing. Out on the river the ferries were still operating for now. Tugboat skippers were also still working, often accompanied by navy warships who were there to guide any merchant vessels lucky enough to get through the blockade. They were bringing vital supplies to the people of our beleaguered nation, yet some of it still found its way to the plates of those who could pay, via the likes of my good friend Percy.

We made it to the Dee Estuary in 45 minutes without incident, and Bill, with the assistance of silent Jim who'd travelled with us, helped the three of us onto a small wooden craft with an outboard motor, they had at first lowered into the calm waters. We were only about 250 yards from the beach and the barbed wire. We could see smoke billowing from the chimney of the safe house but, from our position, it was only possible to see the rooftop. Wilf started up the small outboard motor and steered us to a spot on the beach I'd wondered about the previous day, where I was sure he knew we could break through the wire. Once on the sand, we jumped onto dry land and all three of us dragged the small boat out of the water. Ginny pulled out her piece and ensured there was one in the chamber. She glanced up and down the narrow strip of sand as Wilf picked his spot in the barbed wire, putting on a pair of leather gloves as he peered closely. He then deftly pushed at a section that had been made to look just like the rest of it but was, in fact, an invisible doorway. Once through we followed a path up onto Stanley Road. Ginny pressed her gun against her thigh and I was pleased to see that everything was nice and quiet. Maybe too quiet? I followed Wilf up onto the gravel driveway and I was a little surprised that Toby or Everton hadn't welcomed us inside, as we approached the front entrance.

"Should we worry?"

"Just stop right where you are, gents," Ginny said, and dug two pistols from her bag and pressed them into our hands. "This is no time to get all principled on my ass, Vic."

I simply nodded and looked down at the Colt semi-automatic pistol in my hand, and tried to disguise my disgust. I knew how to use them but promised myself I never would, unless I was backed into a corner.

"You walk around the back, Vic, and we'll go in this way. Fire one shot when you're in position and we'll go in together. If this place has been breached, they might still be inside."

"I assume this isn't protocol, Wilf."

"You assume correctly," he answered, the emotion in his voice betraying his concern.

Wilf didn't argue as Ginny levered him out of the way, so that she could go through the door before him, and I hurried around to the back. They both knew he was no marksman.

I tried to ignore the snakes in my stomach, along with my sweating palms. The gun felt like a slippery foreign body in my hand. Images of Everton, Toby and Agatha lying dead inside tormented my imagination, making it hard to focus. One of the three garage doors was open and I had no idea what this meant. I wiped my free hand on my trousers and fired a single shot into the air. I heard wood splinter and assumed they'd gained entry but, as I hurried inside, I heard no gunshots, no shouting and detected no movement. The air smelled stale and there was an odour I couldn't discern. It wasn't until I reached the small kitchen and saw Everton Cosgrove and Toby unconscious on the linoleum floor, that I realised the problem had perhaps come from within. I looked down at Wilf and Ginny trying to rouse the two stricken men, then turned and raced upstairs to find every room empty. The room that smelled faintly of Agatha's perfume was also vacant, devoid of almost any evidence that it had been recently occupied. I returned to the kitchen and saw that Everton and Toby had come round. They both looked groggy. I looked over at Ginny, who was in the process of dipping her pinkie into one of two teacups on the kitchen counter. I continued to observe as she pushed the same finger into her mouth, her expression turning sour at the taste; she simultaneously pulled her head back just as the substance hit the back of her throat. She didn't know I was watching, or that I'd heard her mutter,

"That fucking bitch."

"You know what was in the tea?"

She turned to face me, her expression revealing the contempt she'd suddenly developed for Agatha Hill.

"I might know you'd be snooping."

"It's what I do."

She looked past me at Wilf, who was still with Toby.

"She only laced their teas with Veronal."

"What the hell is that?"

Wilf shook his head and said in a calm, clear voice, "It's a dangerous barbiturate. Too much of it can be fatal. We can only be grateful she seemed to know how much to administer."

Everton leant forward in his chair and rubbed the back of his neck.

"Friend of Percy's or not, I'll kill her if she crosses my path again," he said, his broken voice lacking its usual lustre, but I knew he meant every word.

Ginny told both men to drink at least three glasses of water each, as she stood over them with her arms crossed. Wilf used the house phone to call a quack on his payroll, while I wondered where the hell the feline had got to and exactly what game she thought she was playing.

*

Doctor Evans arrived. A thin, balding man, wearing horn rimmed glasses and a brown, two-piece suit. He examined both men privately and I took the opportunity to call Percy while I was out of Everton's earshot. I dialled and got him right away, and quickly explained what we'd discovered at the safe house.

"The thing is, Everton means what he says when it comes to killing her. He takes it personally whenever someone tries to rub him out."

"But was she really?

"He heard them say a dose of that stuff can kill and that's enough to convince him."

"So, what are you saying, Vic?"

"We need to keep him out of the way until we can locate Aggie and I have an idea how."

"Go on."

"Wilf is planning to have his man, Toby, taken up to a private nursing home out Formby way. He says he can make room for one more if you can operate without Cosgrove for a week."

"What's this going to cost me?"

"No idea, but what's Aggie's life worth to you?"

"Not as much as it used to be," he said, pausing a couple of beats, "but I think it's a good plan, Vic, please give Wilf the green light and tell him to get them to bill me."

Everton didn't like it but Wilf explained that we'd talked it over with Percy, and he wanted him to get the best care possible. The good Doctor, right on cue, went on to say to both men, that they had to make sure the stuff was completely out of their system.

"Look, Everton, the doc says you're both in the clear, but would it do any harm to let the experts keep an eye on you for the week? Besides, you can relax and put your feet up."

"And consider the many ways Miss Agatha Hill might meet her maker," he said, a sweet and rare smile on his face. Everton wasn't a man to let a thing go easily.

A private ambulance arrived thirty minutes later; the doctor climbed aboard and took Everton and Toby away.

"Let's hope we get this all wrapped up before he's back on the streets," Ginny said.

"Twelve miles or so from civilisation might help with that," Wilf added.

"I wouldn't put it past Cosgrove to break out of there, if his bloodlust overwhelmed him," I added, then thought better of it.

Wilf turned to me, a momentary look of hostility passing across his face.

"Let's not think like that, we're going to have enough trouble tracking her down, without worrying about a gun happy Everton Cosgrove on the loose. Can we drop you off at the marina?"

"Perfect."

We all stepped outside as two more of Wilf's never-ending supply of muscle turned up, in a black Triumph Super 7. Both men looked athletic and light on their feet, dressed in navy overalls; they nodded to Wilf and went inside. Perhaps one of their jobs was to clean the place up and repair the front door, but nobody was fooled. If they were tradesmen, I was related to the King of England himself.

*

The cloud cover overhead had darkened and it looked like it was almost ready to rain. The wind had also whipped up, so I held onto my hat and turned up the collar of my jacket. Some sort of operation was taking place on the river, involving a pair of tugboats and a navy destroyer. They looked to be winching something up out of the gloomy waters. Bill piped up that it might be a mine but, when I looked, I saw it was a body. A male. I'd almost forgotten the numerous young men that had been fished out of the river this year. All young and well dressed. We said very little else during the noisy crossing and it was only as we docked at Wilf's property that he approached me, Ginny by his side.

"We need to find her before she disposes of those pieces, Vic."

"I know."

"I'll make some calls. Get all eyes on it but, perhaps you can try the places she might go. Family? Old friends?"

"I'll do that but, before you say it, I can't see her reaching out to Percy."

"Say she does, are you sure he'll alert you, sugar?" Ginny asked.

"Ginny, I wouldn't have been so sure before her little visit, but trust me on this, something's changed in him. He won't try to shelter her."

"I'm sure you're right, Vic, but we had to ask."

Bill brought *The Windjammer* to a complete stop. I shook Wilf's hand and kissed Ginny. Once on terra firma, I made my way to my office on foot, after refusing the offer of a lift. In all honesty, I wanted some thinking time and only hoped the rain held off until I reached Harry's garage, although I planned to take shelter under the overhead railway if it did, or the docker's umbrella as we liked to call it locally.

*

I was fortunate and reached my office just as the heavens opened. I unlocked the lower door and quickly made my way upstairs. With the rain and the breeze from the river the air had turned cold, so I filled the metal coffee pot with cold water and ground coffee, lit my small stove and set about making myself a proper coffee, in the hope it might warm me. As the good stuff was percolating, I pulled up my venetian blinds and marvelled at the ferocity of the storm. The rain hit Harry's forecourt so hard that it was literally bouncing off in all directions; it created quite a din inside as it pounded the slate roof tiles, only a few feet above me. One thing was for sure, I didn't think the Germans would risk an air raid in this.

I'd given some thought to Aggie's whereabouts and after excluding family, I'd come up with nothing. I racked my brain for any hint from her about who her buyer could be, but she'd clearly decided to go it alone, no longer needing me as muscle it would seem. Perhaps she didn't count on me having friends in high places and knowing anything about the true worth of the *Nine Lives* collection. That said, I still knew hardly anything about why these miniature trinkets, or rather the secret they were hiding, was so sought after.

"Is there enough for two in that coffee pot, Victor?"

I turned and saw Wendy closing a dainty black umbrella. The rain that was now abating had clearly been loud enough to mask the sound of her heels on the stairs.

"This is a rare visit to my inner sanctum," I smiled, pointing to the chair across from my desk. She sat and watched me pour the coffee and bring it over to her, with a bowl of powdered milk and some brown sugar cubes I was saving for a rainy day. I slid into my seat opposite her, raised my cup and sipped mine, before asking how I could help.

"I have a message to deliver, oh great gumshoe."

"I'm all ears."

"You sleuths crack me up, always boasting about some superior skill or other."

I lifted my eyes to the ceiling and shook my head. "Go on."

"With what, lover?"

"The message?"

"Oh that, of course. Two smartly dressed, muscle bound gentlemen, with new haircuts and good manicures were here earlier."

"I can see my natural curiosity and eye for observation is rubbing off on you. What did they want?"

"They were looking for you, handsome. Said they had a job for you but didn't leave any names."

"Didn't or wouldn't?"

"Let's say avoided."

"Say anything else?"

"Not an awful lot. They seemed friendly enough but there's something off about them. None of my business, of course."

"No, it isn't. I appreciate your opinion though."

“Well, for what it’s worth they stank of the service; if they’re not serving military, they used to be.”

“Very interesting, thanks, Wendy.”

Long after Wendy had returned to her own office and the coffee cups and pot had been cleaned and put away, I sat with my feet up on my desk and wondered whether my two visitors had anything at all to do with a certain Miss Agatha Hill.

4

They arrived at ten sharp, next morning. Square jawed, exuding testosterone, their smiles just a little too wide. Exactly how I expected they'd look from Wendy's description.

I knew they might come calling, so I'd got in early and ate an egg sandwich at my desk with a mug of tea. I wanted to prepare for my potential visitors and arrange a few things so that if it went bad, I had a chance to come out of it in one piece. For all I knew they could be the bombers. I spoke to my friend Harry when he arrived at seven. Harry is six foot six in his stocking feet and built like a brick toilet. My expected visitors wouldn't know that he'd lost four toes from his left foot before the war, so I asked him to work a little closer to my office that morning, so that they got a good look at him when they arrived. I also wanted him to clock how they arrived. Whether they were driving or had been dropped off. We'd also worked out a simple signal. Effectively if I needed his help, I would open my window and he'd make his way up the stairs with something like a monkey wrench, or a lump hammer.

I'd also taken the precaution of strapping the blackjack I'd confiscated from a drunken Russian sailor many years before, to my lower right leg. The sailor had been planning to remodel my face that evening. He might have done, had it not been for good fortune and the fact that I can move quick when I need to, plus the help of his friends who dragged him off before he could do any real damage.

I decided I would happily try to replicate the drunken sailor's violent conduct if my prospective customers become threatening.

I looked across at them, meeting their smiles with one of my own. Three shark grins in one tiny office space was perhaps a bit much. I offered them a coffee, which they refused, and asked them how I could help.

The slightly shorter and squatter of the two, who introduced himself as Jones, spoke first. He wasn't local. I could detect no accent at all and that set the alarm bells ringing right away. They were both brown haired and blue eyed, but the talker had a touch of red in his hair.

"We've heard nothing but good things about you, Mr Prince. The word is you're honest, trustworthy, and it seems you're well known in your community."

Community was short for people with similar skin tones to me.

"I don't know whose palms you crossed with silver to get that information, gentlemen, but you make me sound like a saint," I said, offering another beaming smile to those that greeted me.

"We also know you tried to enlist three times and by the looks of you, it's our loss."

"Are you boys in the service then?"

"In a way."

"Is that yes or no?"

"Is that important?"

"It might be. I love my country."

"Then there are only patriots in this room, Mr Prince, and with that in mind we'd like your help tracing someone."

Here it comes, I thought, believing that someone was a certain Miss Agatha Hill.

The taller of the two, who claimed his name was Smith, took over the dialogue but spoke like he worked for the BBC. A little too stiff and plummy for my liking, considering he looked like a weightlifter

"His name is Horatio Afia and up until a fortnight ago he worked with us. It hurts to tell you that he's missing."

"A deserter."

"Some might say absent without leave."

"So that makes you both military policemen?"

They paused, looked at each other and then back at me before Jones took over again.

"Not exactly. You see, we're part of a special unit and we operate remotely from the traditional forces."

I bet you do, I thought.

"What makes you think Mr Afia is in Liverpool?"

"He was born here," Jones went on, "we think he has contacts locally and is keeping his head down. He'll know we're looking for him and that's where you come in, Mr Prince."

Smith reached into an inside pocket and slapped down a photograph of a black man; he had a high forehead and what looked to be a grey streak in his tight curly hair, starting at the left eyebrow and moving across his head from left to right.

"That's Horatio. You can keep that copy, Mr Prince," Smith said.

"Just a minute. I haven't agreed to do anything."

They were like a tag team as Jones took over again.

"Look, we get it, you're a busy man and there is only one of you. We just want you to call us if you hear anything related to Horatio, and for that…"

Smith slapped a wad of cash on my desk next to the table, before picking up exactly where his partner left off. They were like two sides of the same brain and seemingly in perfect sync.

"…shall we say fifty pounds now and fifty when he's found?"

Jones added, "Oh, and if you don't see or hear anything then the cash is yours for your trouble."

They stood, both saluted me and descended the stairs before I could explain that this isn't the way it works, that I have a daily rate and a contract to be signed, before I was prepared to do anything for anyone.

It seemed to me that Jones and Smith, if that was their real names, were either used to bulldozing people in this way, or were playing some sort of long game that I couldn't quite get a handle on. I scratched my head and put the cash away, determined not to touch a penny of it. They struck me as a muscle-bound version of *Tweedledum* and *Tweedledee*.

I descended the stairs and almost bumped into Harry, watching the pair climb into a black cab.

"I suppose that's another dead end," I said.

"Something tells me you're keen to know where this pair might be staying," Harry added, then turned to look at me and asked, "Did they give you any trouble?"

"Not the sort I was expecting. They're hard to read, although I get the impression they're used to getting what they want."

"Fancy a ride?" he asked, raising an eyebrow. "Combined with a little sleuthing?"

I smiled properly for the first time that morning and it felt good.

"Lead the way."

He trotted to a Taylors' bread van, with the keys in the ignition as if he'd planned it this way. As I jumped in beside him and he got us moving, I looked at the vehicle key and then at him.

He saw the look. There was clearly nothing wrong with Harry's peripheral vision.

"You're not the only one who does a little forward planning, Victor."

We trailed them at a safe enough distance, even though we didn't think they'd expect us to even follow them, especially not in a delivery van. The traffic was sparse at first but, as we tracked them into the city centre it grew heavier. We were two cars back when the taxi stopped outside Exchange railway station.

Harry pulled over a couple of hundred yards from the busy entrance, marked by sandbags, and I jumped out.

"I'll wait here, Vic; I'll only slow you down."

I nodded and ran full pelt into the busy station, only slowing as I reached the entrance. The place was filled with uniforms and I scanned it for two grey suits, but saw nothing at first. When I did see them, it was far too late. They'd gone directly to the taxi rank, located near the rear entrance, and had already jumped into another cab and I wondered at first if we'd been spotted or if they were just being over cautious? I opted for the latter, but I could do nothing about it either way.

They were in the wind. There was no way we'd catch them in the one-way system. It was a clever move. So much for thinking ahead.

*

When Harry dropped me back off at my office, my heart sank at the sight of Sergeant Fitzpatrick and his sidekick, Detective Jones, waiting at my door.

I thanked Harry for his help and approached the pair slowly as I dug out my keys, careful not to make eye contact.

"Is this a social call, fellas?"

"We just need a quick word," Jones answered, "but only if you can spare the time, Vic."

I sneaked a look at Fitzpatrick who was finding it hard to play nice by the look of his pie-shaped face; it was turning the colour of a well-cooked gammon. I opened the door and started to go up, then realised neither man had moved, so I shouted over my shoulder,

"Well, come on if you're coming, I haven't got all day."

I was already behind my desk before they made an appearance and I enjoyed a wry smile all the way to my chair. I couldn't quite decide why Fitzpatrick had been told to suddenly start treating me like a member of the human race. Whatever it was, the instruction must have come from higher up and I could see it didn't sit well with him, but I was suddenly starting to enjoy my day.

"Please take a seat and tell me how I can help."

I deliberately directed my question to the Irishman but, once again, it was Jones who found his voice first.

"I'll get right to it, Vic. Did you know that Agatha Hill was back in Liverpool?"

"Why would I?"

"We figured the history she has with Percy etc., you might know."

"She has no reason to contact me, or Percy for that matter. You know their history. It took him more than a year to even look at another woman after she left."

"Understood, Vic. We just wondered if you knew that the night before last, somebody tried to rub her out during an air raid, by chucking explosives into her aunt's place. I think they were hoping to blame the Jerries for the damage."

"Is Aggie alright?"

"That's just it, Vic, we don't know; she hasn't been seen since, according to her father. Look, you don't think Percy would try a stunt like this, do you?"

So that was it, the plods had put two and two together and come up with my best friend.

"Not a chance. My advice is to look into what she's been up to these past two years. I guarantee that'll lead you to your bomber."

Jones sighed heavily.

"Thanks, Vic, but with resources being so scarce we have enough trouble keeping up with what's going on in our own city."

"Is he okay?" I asked, pointing in the direction of Fitzpatrick whose colour had deepened, his face a lather of perspiration.

"No, I'm not, as a matter of fact, Prince. I don't hold with bending and scraping to you and your lot."

I smiled at the venom my goading had unleashed, with just the merest of prods.

"That's more like it, I knew the real you was in there somewhere. It's nice to see you squirm though. Who was it who told you to go against the grain and treat me like a tax paying citizen? Inspector Phillips by any chance?"

"Nobody told us to do anything, you mouthy spade."

"Sergeant, please!" Jones roared across at his colleague.

I banged my fist on the table, my own smile now just a memory.

"It didn't take you long, did it, you racist prick," I said, then I deliberately looked down at my watch. "Your time's up. You can get him out of my office now, Jonesy."

"Come on, Vic, don't be like that."

"And another thing, I don't know who put you up to this but, Fitzpatrick's probably working a side-line, just like he was in the summer, eh, Sergeant?"

"I don't know what this lying coon is saying."

"I think I hit a nerve, Detective. He clearly thinks finding Aggie will earn him a few quid."

"Just tell us where she is, Prince. You know where the bitch is hiding."

"Get him out of here before I remodel his ugly mug."

Jones stood, shook his head, and he was now the one with the red face as they departed without a word. I leaned back in my chair and considered just how they knew about Agatha and her aunt's place.

Wherever they got their information, I was just glad they seemed to know nothing about her movements immediately afterward.

That didn't help me an awful lot though. Agatha was missing and so was the precious cargo she was carrying.

*

The ringing of my office phone interrupted my chain of thought. It was Wilf, explaining that he had men on the lookout for Agatha all over the city. He also updated me on the health of Toby and a certain Everton Cosgrove. They were both doing well but Everton was no longer feeling sorry for himself, having taken a shine to a nurse who hailed from South Africa. Wilf had more class than to ask, but I was in no doubt that he was also expecting an update from me. I told him about my visit from Jones and Smith and how they'd acted extra careful, considering that they never actually knew they were being followed.

"They sound like special ops on the make, Vic."

"Former or current?"

"Who knows, but if they're active now we'll know who they are and where they're stationed. If they've been furloughed for any reason they could be from anywhere."

"Is furloughed a posh word for off duty?"

He laughed.

"No, usually it means they've broken the rules and are on the grey list."

"The grey list?"

“Those with skills we might need to help us win this war, but those who aren’t necessarily squeaky clean. Depending on how far men like that have bent the rules, some would be under lock and key during peacetime.”

“Dangerous then.”

“They’re exactly what we’ve trained them to be. Although as some of the top brass do, we can’t exactly bleat about it when they use those skills for illicit purposes.”

“I suppose not.”

“I’ll see what I can turn up on those two and Afia.”

“The question is, has he double crossed them? Or are they just looking to get in on his action?”

“Impossible to say. So, Agatha Hill never came up?”

“No, and I wasn’t going to introduce her into the conversation. They intimated they selected me to help because Afia and I are both from the same community, meaning black. Sounds too pat to me. They say he’s from the city but I’ve never heard of him. I’ll speak to Percy and my dad. Surely if he is from Liverpool, it’s going to be Toxteth?”

“I grant you it’s rare, but people of colour do occasionally send their children to private schools in this city.”

On that note we ended the call and I promised to drop everything else to concentrate fully on locating Agatha.

5

I was about to head over to Percy's to ask him to put the word out for Afia when the phone rang again. I took off my hat and sat on my desk to answer it, thinking the telephone exchange might have had busier days.

I knew the voice right away from a case I handled up in Southport in the spring. Somebody who ran a bookshop as a cover for helping Wilf out.

"Vic, it's Roderick Peters. I don't suppose a busy man like you will remember this old book worm, son?"

I laughed at that.

"We both know you're much more than a dealer in rare books. Besides, how could I forget a man who saved my hide only this year? I'm assuming this isn't just a social call."

It was his turn to chuckle.

"Not at all, I'm sorry to say. Wilf asked me to keep an eye on your associates and it was a shrewd call, Vic."

I stood in unison with the hairs on the back of my neck that were suddenly proud.

"Go on."

"I followed your friend Jimmy to a tea shop on Lark Lane, where he met a very attractive young woman, but I wasn't the only one who had him under observation."

"Where are you now?"

"I'm speaking from a place we use above the Post Office, in Lark Lane. I don't think I've been clocked but I'm keeping an eye on the man watching."

"White man, suit bulging with muscle."

"From the back that just about describes him, although I don't have the clearest of views. He is waiting in the back of a black cab with the meter running, must be costing him a fortune."

"I'm on my way over."

"Then come in the back way. You'll see a green door, hit the buzzer three times but leave a beat between each ring, and I'll buzz you through."

"Seems like I owe you another."

"Nobody's counting, Vic."

I put my hat on, checked my keys were in my pocket and made my way downstairs.

Harry waved from the bonnet of an old Wolsey as I locked the door. I turned to go but the smell of strong alcohol met my flared nostrils. Fitzpatrick had returned alone and shuffled so close on his bad leg that we were almost chest to chest. I looked down at him, sneering.

"What do you want now?"

Harry stopped what he was doing and watched. He knew the disdain Fitzpatrick and I had for each other.

"I have it on good authority that you're shielding that black bitch and her cargo."

"Who told you that, the barman who was pouring your cheap whiskey?"

"You never mind how I know what I know. My contact is prepared to offer you a finder's fee to get those items she's carrying."

I flattened my hand and put it out in front of me, and walked him back a few steps. Harry dropped a wrench and stepped in our direction.

"For starters, I'm not partial to your breath polluting my personal space. Secondly, even if I did know where Agatha is, which I don't, you're the last man in Liverpool I'd tell. Oh, and you can tell your contact to shove his money."

"This is your last chance to come clean, Prince. I'm warning you."

I laughed in his face.

"What are you going to do, cry? Go on, knock yourself out."

His colour was deepening and he lumbered towards me again, but he was stopped by Harry who got in between us and smiled down at his diminutive frame.

"This could be construed as police harassment, Sergeant. Do you know I look after Inspector Philips' car for him?"

That seemed to sober him up. He wiped his mouth with the back of his hand and looked past Harry, at me.

"Take note. I have eyes on you, Prince. I'll have that licence off you one of these days."

"I'm quaking in my shoes, Sergeant."

He turned and limped off, muttering as he went.

I pushed my hat to the back of my head.

"Two visits from Fitzpatrick in one day is enough for anyone," I said, then patted Harry on the arm and thanked him for intervening.

*

Lark Lane is a stone's throw from Sefton Park, Liverpool's biggest green space, with the park at one end and the busier Aigburth Road at the other. It was a place where artists and chilled out individuals congregated as a rule. There was the Albert Hotel, which was a genuine hotel back then and not just a pub. There was also a tea-room run by a local herbalist, a busy post office, where Roderick waited, a couple of eateries and a variety of smaller businesses. I assumed Jimmy and his lady friend fancied a walk through the park after a bite to eat and, as I looked up at a brightening sky, I thought they just might find others with the same idea.

I jumped on the overhead railway and got off at my usual stop at the end of the line, which just happened to be the Dingle. I could walk it from there. I often took myself off to the park when I needed to think and Lark Lane was a little closer.

I found the green door, buzzed as instructed and was admitted by a slightly greyer looking Roderick Peters. He couldn't have looked less like one of Wilf's boys if he tried. He wore a navy cardigan over a white shirt and red dickie bow, and I saw that a grey-flecked goatee had grown on his lower jaw since our last meeting. I knew from personal experience, that his disarming appearance could be deceiving. I'd witnessed his skill with a firearm for myself, in the garden of a ruthless Italian we butted heads with, when our paths last crossed.

We shook hands and he asked me to follow him up a narrow staircase.

He had a flask of tea, smokes and two comfy chairs, plus a small table to the left of the offending window. He moved to the right and beckoned me to stand beside him, and I could just about make out Jimmy in uniform and the svelte Gloria Potter, who these days worked for Mei-Li at The White Oyster club. They were seated in the window of the aptly named The Tea Rooms, all smiles and deep in conversation, oblivious to our presence. Immediately below, I saw the profile of Mr Jones, the slightly smaller of my two morning visitors. I told Roderick about my morning visitors and what they wanted from me.

We stepped back and he reached for a cigar, offering me one. I refused and he lit his up.

"Why Jimmy?"

"I think they're executing standard conventions, namely they're watching as many of your friends as they can, hoping you'll lead them to the person or persons they're looking for."

"So why go through the rigmarole of hiring me?"

Roderick sat and offered me a restrained smile.

"Percentages, Vic, and the element of surprise," he said as I peeked outside again, to see that nothing had changed. "They reckon if you don't know where Afia is you soon will. If you find him, they'll use you as a cover to move in on him."

"I almost told them to stick their money where the sun don't shine and didn't agree to anything."

"That won't make any difference, they've done their homework on you, Vic, and know how well connected you are. They might also assume you'll be curious about Afia and of them for that matter. If that's the case they'll want to be ready. There is of course one other possibility."

"Go on."

"They might know you're working with Wilf."

I nodded and thought he made a good point.

"You said there were two of them?"

"I did."

"Then my guess is his partner is following up other leads."

I didn't say anything, but I immediately wondered who Smith might have his peepers on.

I thought I saw movement out of the corner of my eye and sure enough, Jimmy was paying his bill. Jones also saw that and made moves to pay off his driver.

"Jimmy's on the move."

In a flash Roderick had his coat and hat on and said,

"I've got this covered, Vic, besides, you'll stick out like a sore thumb and he knows you. I'll update you later, just pull the door closed when you leave and it'll auto-lock."

I stood and watched Jimmy and his girl stroll towards the park, ignorant to the fact that he was being watched by not one, but two trained killers.

*

When I got to Percy's my father answered the door, which was unusual.

"Come in, son, I suppose you can give us a hand."

"With what?" I asked.

He didn't respond but headed for the stairs, and I followed him up to a part of the house I hardly ever ventured into. We headed to Percy's room where I saw that my friend was lying diagonally, spread eagled, on his king size bed, fully dressed but his clothing was in disarray. A smile adorned his face and his eyes stared up at the ceiling, as if it was the most interesting thing he'd ever seen in his life. He was singing a bawdy, local song at the top of his lungs.

"...put it in the back not the front, said the coalman, throw your balls in the air, said the juggler, merry, merry men are we..."

Paul stood on the other side of the bed facing us, with his arms crossed, his chest heaving.

"We've tried to undress him and get him into his bed but it's like trying to wrestle a tiger."

I removed my hat and jacket, lifted my still singing friend off the bed and held him close to me, so that he couldn't move, as Paul and my father successfully took off his clothing. They then pulled back the sheets, blanket and thick eiderdown and I rolled him into bed, tucking him under the covers as tight as I was able. By the time we tip-toed out of the room he was snoring.

When we were downstairs, I told my dad and Paul to grab a seat in the front parlour while I made a strong pot of the good coffee. I carried it in on a tray with three beef dripping sandwiches and as we ate and drank, I asked about Percy.

"It's that girl, Victor. He's concerned for her safety and he pretends he no longer has the same feelings for her, and maybe he doesn't, but he feels something."

I knew Paul was right, but I didn't feel it'd serve any purpose to go on about Percy's emotions.

"Was he like that when you got here?"

"I was supposed to drive him over to a new warehouse he's setting up, over near Bramley Moore dock, but I found him pie eyed in the kitchen, sitting on one those damn bar stools. If I'd have arrived ten minutes later, I guarantee he'd have fallen and split his damn head open."

"How come you're here, Dad?"

"Percy had a phone installed for us, so Paul called and asked me to walk across and give him a hand. I was better than useless though; my muscles are so wasted it's a miracle I can stand."

"Don't be like that, you got him upstairs after all."

Before we could discuss it any further, Percy's hall telephone chirped into life and Paul, as the only employee of my drunken friend in the room, took it upon himself to answer it. He walked back in almost immediately and said,

"It's Frank Robins and he wants to talk to you, Vic."

"Why me?"

"It's about something Percy asked him to do."

Frank, like almost all of Percy's men, fought in the first war but was considered too old to fight in this one. He was one of Percy's warehouse managers who lived up in Waterloo, way up in the north coast.

I went to take the call.

"Hello, Frank, what can I do for you?"

"Percy asked me to speak to my contacts in the hotel trade, up where I live. He told me to ask my pals to keep an eye out for a well-dressed black female, and guess what?"

"You found her?"

"It's her alright. Not too many people of colour come this far north of the city, so she was likely to stand out. She's staying in a fleapit of a place up in Thornton and hasn't come out of her room since she arrived, other than to use the shared facilities."

I wrote down the address and thanked him, assuring him Percy would be as pleased as punch. Although I didn't add, once he'd sobered up.

I went back into the room and told them the good news. Paul offered to drive me over there, while my dad said he'd stay and keep an eye on Percy.

"I don't suppose either of you have ever heard of Horatio Afia?"

They both shook their heads.

"Who is he?" Paul asked.

"He's supposed to be from these parts."

"Never heard of him," my dad said.

"Charles and I would know him, or his family, if they were from Toxteth. Are you sure he's from around here?"

"It's what I was told. I was obviously misinformed."

As we were about to leave, Jimmy walked through the door, looking rather pleased with himself. I was glad no harm had come to him. I quickly filled him in and he said he'd tag along, then quickly went to get his service revolver.

I hoped we wouldn't need it.

6

Paul went out to the car and I said I needed a word with Jimmy, and that we'd follow him out in a minute or so.

I caught up with him in his room and quickly explained about Jones and Smith, and the fact that Roderick had called me when he spotted Jones tailing him.

"Christ, Vic, who are those guys?"

"I don't know for sure but I'm working on it. One thing is certain, they have a high opinion of themselves and think they can buy and sell us. That just might work to our advantage."

"Thanks for looking out for us anyway."

"You can thank Wilf when you see him. He knows how these types work."

He found his gun and on our way out to the car, I said,

"You kept the date with Miss Potter quiet."

"You know women can't resist me, Vic, what can I say?"

"Sure, you're the Yiddish Rudolph Valentino himself."

"More like the Jewish Long John Silver."

That tickled us both and we were still chuckling when we climbed into the white Rolls.

"Did I miss something?"

"Just James Cohen, lady killer."

"I see, glad I missed that then."

Paul's comments set us off again as he started up the engine and got us moving.

Thornton was a small village to the north east of Crosby and I wondered what had made

Agatha risk travelling to such a remote location, where she'd stand out like a sore thumb. My only conclusion was that she must have been meeting somebody who'd insisted upon the locale.

The hotel was a plain, rectangular, sandstone structure that had seen better days. Unlike some hotels in the area I don't suppose it could afford to be too choosy. Those were the type with aspirations of attracting a more affluent customer. Some posted a sign that simply said, 'No Irish, no blacks, no dogs.'

This place was called The Grand and I assumed the name was some sort of gag. The place couldn't have been less grandiose if it tried. We parked opposite on a nice quiet street, with few cars about, but as we exited our vehicle, somebody started to take pot shots at us. I pulled Paul to the ground and Jimmy ducked, going down on his good knee beside our sprawled bodies. Pulling out his army issue Browning sidearm, he scanned the hotel windows.

"Fourth floor, third from the left."

Paul and I joined Jimmy, down on our haunches, and I saw that the window he referred to was open, although the shooting had stopped. The faded net curtains hid whoever was behind them.

"Agatha, you think?"

"Has to be, Jim."

"Why is she shooting at us?"

"I suppose she's telling us she wants to sell those pieces her way."

"I don't suppose you brought a gun, Vic?"

I shook my head and grimaced.

"If you want to make a run for the door, I could make some noise with this."

"Is it worth the risk, Vic?" Paul asked. "And if you do get over there, and you're not full of holes, what do you do against the shooter when you get inside?"

"She wouldn't shoot me."

"That's assuming it is her."

I knew Paul was right but I also knew the longer we waited, we risked the chance that someone would call the authorities. Salvation, if I could call it that, came in the form of the air raid siren. We waited until guests started to exit in search of shelter. A stick thin man, who looked to be in charge, wearing a pale blue suit, and sporting a pencil thin moustache, spoke to those gathered at the front and did a quick head count. He knew the count was short; he looked up at the open window and shook his head, before leading his party to an Anderson shelter, situated on some waste ground adjacent to the place.

"I say you and me go in, while this is all going off. Paul, you'd be safer in the shelter."

"If you're going inside, I'm coming with you."

There was no time to argue. We could hear the sound of bombs falling in the distance as we ran across the road. Jimmy fired three shots in the direction of the open window and we moved.

I burst through first. Jimmy was slower because of his false leg, just below the left knee, attached to what remained of his left leg, and Paul's best running days were behind him. I stopped for a second, listening for any noises that might indicate somebody armed and dangerous was heading my way. I noted that there was no elevator. The foyer was small and cramped, and a staircase that led to the upper floors looked to be the only way up or down. The others joined me by the time I'd got the layout of the place, and we made our way up to the fourth floor as the siren continued to sound. The bombs were dropping further up the coast, targeting the docks, so we didn't feel as though we were in imminent danger.

The stairs creaked like old bones but, fortunately there was enough background noise to mask it, or so we hoped. Jimmy had his gun out in front, but Paul and I only had our eyeballs protruding.

We reached our destination without incident and turned left into a narrow corridor of closed doors. Jimmy counted them down and when he reached what we all agreed must be Agatha's room, he turned the doorknob and it swung inward.

On the floor of the room was a big man in a dark grey suit, with skin the same shade as mine. He'd been shot in the back and Jimmy covered me as I rolled him over and felt for a pulse. I saw a grey streak in his hair and his face matched a photograph I'd recently been given.

"Dead," I said.

I went through his pockets and found a Walther pistol and a wallet, but nothing else. In the wallet was fifty-four pounds and fifteen shillings. Also, there was a pawn shop ticket and what looked like a front door key, plus a black and white photograph. I put most of it away in my own pockets and then took a closer look at the grainy snap. The deceased was standing between two white men. All three were in uniform and when I saw the faces of the two men flanking him, I was in no doubt that this was the body of Horatio Afia. I stood and explained my theory to my two friends.

“This ties Jones and Smith to Agatha. So, I have to assume they were hoping Afia would lead them to her.”

“Do you think Aggie did this?”

“It doesn’t make sense, Jim,” I replied. “If Afia was who she was meeting, why kill him?”

“What if she was meeting somebody else and Afia followed them here?” Paul piped up.

“Either way, I’d say Agatha and at least one other person could still be in the building, and in my opinion, they’ll be armed.”

“So how do we play this?” Jimmy asked.

“This is definitely Aggie’s room. There’s a whiff of her perfume in here. I say you and Paul stay here and search the room. No offence, Jim, but I move quicker than you if I have to.”

I picked up the gun and felt the burn of acid in my stomach, at the feel of the cold steel in my hand. Before I set off, I checked it was loaded and touched the brim of my hat to my friends who wished me luck. I headed back the way we’d come in. The stairwell was at the centre of one long corridor, so at first, I chose to check there were no surprises at the far end of the fourth floor. Every door was locked and I knew because I checked all of them, and listened as I moved along the thinning carpet on the balls of my feet, ready to move at pace if I had to. I knew once the all clear sounded the other guests would head back in, but it was no excuse to get careless.

I moved back to the stairs and listened. I heard something and stood stock still and tried to listen for movement, in spite of the persistent wailing of the siren.

My patience rewarded me, as I picked up on the faint sound of footsteps and something else I couldn't quite identify. I stood stock still and closed my eyes.

There it was again, something like a popping sound, but not loud enough to be gunfire.

Then there was a crash, as if something had been dropped or thrown, but I couldn't be sure whether the noise came from the floor above or below. I was running out of time so I took a punt on the floor below, assuming that somebody might have been trying to leave before being cornered. By the time I'd reached the lower corridor, I knew my fifty-fifty toss of the coin had paid off.

I knew that noise. A fight was taking place. I moved into a trot and turned right. The sound of two people going at it grew louder. I stopped and made sure there was a bullet in the chamber, then peeked around an open door.

Inside, a blonde man, in a tan suit who had lost his hat, was being held by a broader man wearing a navy suit and a flat cap. Beside them was a curtain on the floor. That could have explained the popping sound, as it had been wrenched out of its fastenings. The broader man's neck was peacock red, just like the taller man's face. Our eyes locked as he pushed the other man off him. He glanced up at me and back at the other man, who was advancing on him.

"Hey," he shouted, causing the bulkier man to glance over his shoulder. It was a clever move, as he took the man's momentary hesitation to send his elbow hard into his jaw, and then I saw it. On the floor not ten feet from where they stood, was another pistol. It looked like a Colt semi- automatic, black paint job with a brown handle. I knew it was used by the US military as a sidearm. He dived for it but I was two steps away, and back heeled it behind me. The blonde looked pissed and then even more irritated, when the other bloke got to his feet and sent a kick into his midriff.

"That's enough!" I roared, just as he was about to try another kick. He ignored me, so I fired my pistol into the ceiling. That got his attention. "I said, that's it, pal, or the next one is in your skull."

"Who the fuck are you?" Blondie asked in a neutral accent that could easily have been classroom earned. He was now on his feet, his chest heaving.

"I might ask you two the same."

They both just glared at me.

"Okay then, up against the wall, both of you, face forward, legs apart."

"Don't tell me you're the old bill."

"Non impiegherebbero un negro," he said, laughing.

The stockier one was speaking Italian and I got part of what he was saying. He was doubting I was police because of my complexion and he might have had a point.

They did as I asked and I patted them both down. I found a stiletto blade in a special holster, strapped to the Italian's calf, and knuckle dusters in the inside of Blondie's tan jacket.

"Now, I'm prepared to play nice, but I want to know what the Yanks and the Italians are doing sending agents to this Godforsaken place?"

The room was suddenly silent as the air raid siren briefly ceased. I was running out of time as any minute, the all clear was about to sound.

"Last chance. This place is going to be crawling with hotel guests and, pretty soon after, the real boys in blue, so unless somebody talks, I'll hand you both over to them. There's a dead man upstairs, which one of you gutless wonders put a bullet in his back?"

They were either both very good actors or genuinely surprised, by the looks on their faces, which made me wonder whether I had everything the wrong way around.

"If it wasn't one of you two, who was it?"

I heard footsteps approaching. Whoever it was, was good. I almost didn't hear the creaking floorboards, just before the all clear started to ring out.

"Look, throw me that gun, I won't use it on you, I promise." Blondie was almost pleading, a petrified look in his eye.

"What is it?" was all I recall saying, before a searing pain engulfed me and the floor opened up and swallowed me whole. As I fell forward into a chasm of pain, I heard gunshots and the last thing I remember thinking was, well, at least the pain'll stop.

It did, as the comfort of darkness overwhelmed me.

*

I saw Jimmy's face first. I was sitting up and I could see the thin man in the blue suit, worriedly fingering his moustache. We were in somebody's cramped office and Paul shoved a glass in my hand. I put my nose to the contents and the smell of the cheap hooch almost made me throw up.

"How are you feeling, son?" Paul asked.

"Like I've been pulled inside out, after they stomped on my head for a day or so."

Jimmy smiled.

"He's alright, or he wouldn't be trying to make jokes."

"What do you mean, trying?"

They both chuckled this time.

"Somebody take this off me before my lunch makes a swift reappearance."

Paul turned my face toward his and it was then I realised he was seated beside me.

"The manager has called the local police, so we need to wait and talk to them."

I nodded and as I did, my head felt like it was made of cast iron.

"It's a real shit show up there, Vic. They found you in a room with two dead men and guess what, the gun you had on you smelled like it had been fired."

That woke me up.

"So that's it, whoever did this only let me live so I could carry the can for all three."

"Look, if you can walk, can I suggest we get out of here before the plod arrive? They'll take one look at your black faces and decide you're both guilty, even before they realise that gun you were holding was fired," Jimmy said.

"Where is the piece?"

"I put in back in Horatio's pocket," Jimmy said in a low voice, so that the hotel manager didn't hear him.

Paul had a different view.

"Come on, Jimmy, if we leave now, how long do you think it'll take them to figure this out? I vote we stay and take our chances, and play your trump card if it doesn't go well."

I knew he meant Wilf and I realised I'd need to call him with an update anyway.

We would never have made it as it turned out. In walked a heavy set man, with copper written all over his face. He looked to be in his fifties, in a well cut navy suit, and was about my height. He had a pock marked face, and strode inside with a man who looked older than God himself, replete with snow white locks and a face so lined, it looked like old leather. I looked at the younger man's grey eyes and was hopeful, they looked sharp and intelligent.

He spoke to the manager and then went off to look at the bodies, as a uniformed constable stood guard in the doorway, occasionally looking at Paul and I, like something he might find on the bottom of his shoe.

The big man returned, his expression unreadable as he spoke to the hotel manager again.

The constable led Paul and Jimmy outside and I found myself alone with the two detectives.

"My name's Gradwell, this is Petersson. He retired five years ago but he's a patriot."

They were both Inspectors, but it seemed that that the younger man outranked the retired version.

I hoped I hadn't read him wrong, so I went through my three attempts to enlist and my alleged flat feet and mild asthma, given as the reason I was not deemed fit.

"You don't buy it?"

"Not a bit of it."

I told him my name and what I did for a living.

"This was work related, your being here today, I mean?"

"It was."

"Before we get into any of that, let me save us all a little time. Henrik here is a known associate of one Wilfred Henderson. Before he rejoined the force he did some private work for Mr Henderson, who he says speaks highly of you, Mr Prince. So, despite what you may have initially thought, you're among friends here."

I felt my shoulders visibly relax.

"Call me Vic."

"Vic, I'm Richie."

"Call me Hank," Petersson said, smiling, but those bluer than blue eyes saw eveything. Then he turned to his partner wearing a look of mock disappointment, "Henrik, indeed."

"Have you spoken to Wilf recently, Hank?"

"If you're asking me if I know what you're working on, then the answer is a firm no."

I smiled and spread my hands.

"I don't suppose you'd be offended if I spoke to Wilf before I spill what I know?"

It was Gradwell who answered for both men.

"There's a perfectly servicable telephone right in front of us. Knock yourself out, Vic. What the hotel don't know won't hurt them."

I dialled as Gradwell fired up a Lucky Strike and Petersson a clay pipe. They watched and listened in silence, as I told Wilf very little other than where I was and who I was with. He asked me to pass the phone to Hank, who took it willingly and mostly listened, puffing out clouds of fragrant smoke from his pipe.

When the call ended, Gradwell narrowed his eyes and asked,

"We good?"

"We are."

"Okay then, off you go."

I told them about the search for Agatha, leaving out the bombing at her aunts and mentioned nothing about the *Nine Lives.* Although I spoke about Jones and Smith, and how I thought one of the dead men upstairs was a man they tried to hire me to find.

"So, let me get this straight, you've no idea who popped those three but you're not excluding this woman, Agatha?"

"That's about right."

"Thanks for the that, Vic, now we have something for you. Whether it's relevant or not I couldn't say," he said, stubbling out his second smoke of the session. "We got word that some sort of auction was supposed to take place here tonight."

So that was what Miss Agatha was up to. It also explained why there seemed to be different factions present, and I didn't doubt that the place was literally crawling with potential buyers, even those with links to the enemy, such as the now dead Italian.

"Did your information mention what was up for sale?"

Gradwell sat back and for the first time he sensed I was holding out on him.

"I thought you'd be able to tell us that."

I barked out a dry, sarcastic laugh.

"If I did they'd lock me in irons and throw away the key. Trust me, you don't want to know. This goes all the way to the big, cigar smoking chief."

"Fair enough, Vic. How else can we help?"

"You could keep all eyes on any sighting of Agatha Hill," I said and gave them her description, then added, "I don't think she'd be too hard to spot in these parts."

"Is there any reason to think she'd stay around here?" Hank asked.

"I wish I knew the answer to that."

"I think we're all good here then, Vic, and remember, you've got friends in the north if you ever need them."

"More than I have in the south, on the force anyway," I quipped.

Gradwell smiled for the first and only time as he shook my hand, followed by Petersson.

"You can't be referring to a certain ginger haired detective sergeant, with a chip on his shoulder as wide as the Irish sea."

It was my turn to smile.

"The one and only," I said and thanked them again before leaving.

*

Jimmy and Paul were astonished that I'd just waltzed out of there and even more surprised when we were all allowed to leave, as they were both expecting the third degree. They followed me outside. We got to the car and Paul started it up, but it wasn't until we'd fought our way out of the narrow streets of Thornton that they pumped me for information.

"Well, Vic, do tell how we all avoided the thumb screws. And don't try and convince us you talked your way out of that one," Jimmy added.

I offered him a weak smile.

"Not what you'd expect. The older of the two knew Wilf."

"So, somebody up there likes you after all."

"Seems that way. Except that someone took my wallet, along with Afia's, after I was knocked out cold."

"I thought a man in your business would know better than to carry his cash in his wallet," Paul piped up.

I grinned into the rear view mirror and responded,

"I didn't say there was any cash in it."

I then disclosed what I'd been told about an apparent auction of the pieces Agatha was holding.

"Did we arrive too late?"

"I hope not, Jim. But it's clear our trip has provided more questions than answers."

Jimmy nodded as Paul also stayed silent. It give me a chance to do some thinking of my own. I started by making a mental list composed of the new questions our trip had thrown up. The first was, why was Afia killed and what role was he taking in the auction? Then I wondered, was I really spared to take the fall? What if the killer was my closest friend's ex-fiancee? Finally, and probably most important of all, where was Agatha and was she still holding the *Nine Lives*?

We finally arrived back at Percy's as dusk was falling. My dad informed me that the man of the house hadn't stirred.

"He'll have one hell of a headache when he eventually wakes up though."

I laughed and went to call Wilf. I filled in the gaps following our brief conversation earlier and walked him through my list of questons. He agreed with my assessment and all he said was,

"We need to find her, Vic."

"Like yesterday."

"Vic, before you go, there is something else I need to tell you."

His words made my blood run cold.

"Go on."

"Ginny has been keeping an eye on your place and guess what?"

"Laurel and Hardy have turned up?"

"Not exactly how I'd refer to them," he said and I could hear him inhale his smoke. "Smith and Jones to be precise, but she wanted me to tell you she isn't alone and they have the situation under control."

"I'm going over there now."

"Go in softly, Vic."

"I will, right until I get my hands on those two clowns."

I said my goodbyes and faked my mood, not wanting to worry my father. When I got outside, a cool wind had whipped up and I turned up the collar of my jacket and pulled down the brim of my hat. It was pitch black, so I stayed in the shadows but moved as fast as I could. The last thing I needed was the ARP warden collaring me. I was a ball of nervous energy and it wouldn't be a good thing if he did, as I was liable to knock him on his backside. Jones and his partner had crossed the line coming near my family and, while I knew Ginny could handle them, a combination of anger and worry coarsed though my veins, as I hurried into the Autumn night.

7

I eventually navigated the ink black streets and was closing in on my first floor flat, when an arm reached out of the darkness and tugged at my forearm. I almost jumped out of my skin, but the arm quickly released me and I was relieved to see Ginny's face. She'd flicked on a torch that she was pressed under her chin, the result was slightly macabre, showing her lovely face in a ghostly pose, then I watched an index finger move to her lips to silence me. She wore a trouser suit, with a white shirt, dark tie and a fedora on her pretty head and signalled that I should follow. I did, just after she plunged us back into darkness and she crept forward slowly, as I hung onto her coat-tails.

The rear of my place opens onto a rectangular forecourt and two back entries. Other than that, a solitary street fed into this rather out of the way place. The rear of the many properties butting up to the boundary were dark and quiet. Ginny put her lips to my ear and her words tickled as she spoke,

"They're standing alone at the mouth of each alley. I've been able to get a man in behind them. When you're ready, walk out there as if you're going home, but take it nice and slow and when they approach, we'll move in. Nod if you agree."

I nodded and held my thumb up. I took a few deep breaths Ginny sensing the emotions that were swirling inside of me, rubbed my upper arm. I took a few more lungs full of the cooling night air and strode out into the empty courtyard. When I got close I deliberately slowed my gait, as if fumbling for my keys, just below a few short steps that led to the door I always used to come and go. I heard their light footsteps approach and gritted my teeth. I wanted nothing more than to swivel ninety degrees and bang their heads together. I could almost taste the violence, my imagination yearned to unleash on the two men.

Then I felt it. The barrel of a gun press into the small of my back.

"Easy Vic, we come in peace."

I raised my arms slowly and said nothing, instead concentrating on keeping my feet planted on the pavement and my hands off the two goons, attempting to push me into some play they thought they'd executed so well.

"You may come in peace but we don't."

Ginny's voice was like a salve and when I turned I saw the sour expressions on the faces of Jones and Smith. Ginny's men were large shadowy figures in the poor light, with their own guns pointed at the two, who now had their hands up, just as mine were. Ginny flicked on her powerful torch and delibaratety shone a thin beam of light into their eyes, moving back and forth between the two. They squinted and complained and I stepped forward.

"I think they call that check mate fellas."

They said nothing.

Ginny eventually lowered the flashlight.

"What exactly do you two cheese dicks think you're up to? I think your egos were running this play."

I took the guns off them, dropped them to the ground and backheeled them behind me. I then patted them both down and emptied their pockets of smokes, cash, my wallet and Afia's, which I found in the pocket of Smith.

"You know I was up at the grand hotel in Thornton earlier today Ginny and get this, somebody hit me hard enough to put out my lights permanently and to make matters worse, when I woke up my wallet was gone. Any ideas who hit me Mr Smith?"

More silence.

I moved close enough to smell him.

"I have to assume the man holding my wallet is the same coward who backshot Afia and killed those two unarmed men."

"You don't know what you're talking about," he eventually said, then attempted to push me away, placing his open palm on my chest. I was angry now and swung my right arm in an upward motion, not only knocking his hand off me, but backhanding him in the process. I was pleased with the whip I got. He staggered back into the man behind him, who was alert enough to keep him upright.

"Are you just going stand to there and let this monkey assault us?" Jones piped up.

His words were a plea to Ginny. In a way he was really saying, we're the same and you're not supposed to let him to that to one of your own.

"Vic can strip and pistol whip the pair of you for all I care. What do you expect? You've had his friends followed all over the city, and now you have the gaul to come to his home. Is nothing sacred to you two? Apparently not. As I see it, you boys have crossed the line and you have to accept the consequences."

"This is war, there are no lines. You know that better than anyone here," Jones spat back at her."

"If you two are fighting the good fight, which I doubt, aren't we all on the same side?" I asked.

They clammed up again.

"Vic, either you've hit a nerve or they're dumb struck by your incredible powers of deduction."

"They're not dumb struck, just plain dumb. If the slugs in those guns match the ones found in any one of the three men killed up north earlier today, you two are finished. War or no war, you'll be going inside for a long time."

"My man has a contact in the department investigating those murders," Ginny added, "so I think you gents will be joining us, at least until we can straighten all of this out. Cuff 'em boys."

They struggled but the men bearing down on them were bigger and stronger and fastened their hands behind their backs with ease.

"This is an outrage," Smith squeeled.

"We shot nobody, its Agatha you want for this."

"Tell us where she is boys and we'll happily ask her." Ginny answered.

"Do you think if we knew that we'd be here."

"At least that answers a question that's been nagging at me, from the moment you two stepped into my office," I said, "you were after her all along."

“Get them out of my sight,” Ginny instructed her men, as she knelt and scooped up their pistols.

“Hold on,” I said, and reached down into my sock and retrieved a wad of cash and stuffed it into the inside pocket of Jones’s jacket, “take your money and don’t ever come anywhere near my friends, or family again. If you do, it’ll be more than a slap you’ll get next time.”

“And I might not be here to save your sorry hides,” Ginny quipped before they were dragged away and marched off into the darkness.

She turned to me.

“You okay big guy?”

“I am now and no small thanks to you. This has been a big waste of everyone’s time. You should be at home in front of the fire with that man of yours.”

She chuckled.

“You’re assuming I can drag him away from his desk.”

“Don’t give me that, we both know you’re a shrewd operator, I’m sure you have a few tricks up your sleeve.”

She laughed again then deftly changed the subject.

“Do you buy what Jones said about Agatha killing those men?”

“She’s more than capable but I don’t see her killing two unarmed men, or shooting anybody in the back for that matter. Those three killings look like the work of a profesional. Those two fit the profile alright, but let’s assume they didn’t kill anyone today, why was Smith holding my wallet?

Not to mention the one belonging to a dead man, backshot at the grand?"

"If it isn't them, then they're working with the killer?"

"No flies on you Ginny. While you're holding them, maybe you can persuade them to talk?"

She laughed again but sardonically.

"You obviously know nothing about how these types are trained. We'll get nothing out of them that way. Our best bet is to find out where they've been staying and go through their stuff, and ask around to try and get descriptions of who they've been seen with. We assumed they were working for themselves but what if they are in cahoots with someone?"

"Or more likely on someone's payroll."

Even in such poor light, I noticed a queer expression on her face and didn't realise it at first, but I now know it was concern.

"Can you describe the men who were killed today?"

I did and she gritted her teeth, shook her head, then took a deep breath.

"You know them?"

"One of them. I'm pretty sure the blonde man was Jake Lundstrom. We both worked for John Smith. He was such great guy."

"That's means he was US secret service?"

"Afraid so."

"Sorry it was your friend Ginny."

She nodded and tried to force the corners of her mouth into an upward curve. It was a valiant effort.

"Well we won't learn anything else standing around in the cold. I'm going to get those two squared away, while you give your woman a hug."

She planted a kiss on my cheek, then disappeared into the night with a heavy heart. I was more grateful to her than I could say. She was one of the smartest people I'd ever met and there was nobody tougher in my book. We were lucky she was on our side.

*

I gave myself a moment and it was one of the few times I can ever remember being sorry that I didn't have a smoke in my pocket. Mei-Li was somebody who picked up on nuances and I didn't want to give away any hint whatsoever that she'd been in danger. I stood there letting my breathing return to normal and by the time I stepped up to the door and unlocked it, the tips of my fingers were cold.

My girl was putting in her earrings with her back to me, a beautiful and fragrant silhouette in a midnight blue dress, that hugged the contours of her petite frame, and I swear it could not have looked better on anyone else on the planet.

She turned and her lovely face greeted me.

"Can you fix yourself something to eat? I have to dash in ten minutes or so."

It was one of her nights at the White Oyster club, a basement jazz club, run by our friend Carlos.

"I'm coming with you," I said. I took off my hat and dropped it into a chair, and kissed her on the lips, "I'll quickly change."

I walked to my wardrobe, picked out a fresh suit, and laid it on the bed, then went to a sink we have behind a bamboo screen and washed in cold water but with the fancy soap, courtesy of Percy.

"What about food Vic? You must be starving."

"I'll grab a bite at the club."

I dressed quickly, then dug out my lightweight overcoat, and stepped from behind the screen to retrieve my hat, as Mei-Li wriggled into her own woollen coat.

"You might need a neck scarf it's cool out there now."

"I'm tougher than I look," she told me and winked.

"I already know that," I said, smiling and doing my best to keep the conversation light I quipped, "come on then hard case, let's get you to work."

We walked out into the deserted forecourt, that had recently been brimming with testosterone and the equally robust Ginny Merrill. I pushed it out of my mind as I told Mei-Li about the state we found Percy in, but nothing about the three dead men up north, or the rather large bump on the back of my head for that matter.

We made it to the club on the dark, desolate streets and as we got inside, there was quite a crowd building up already in the foyer, waiting to hand in their coats and hats, and as we walked through to the empty room the band were tuning up. I spotted Gloria putting the finishing touches to the tables. She winked at me and I wondered whether Jimmy had told her that I knew about them. Mei-Li kissed me and went off to gather her troops together for a quick word. I turned to see Carlos polishing glasses on the bar.

"Business is good I see?"

"Can't complain. When death may be just around the corner, people like to have a good time my friend," he smiled and came around the bar to hug me, pecking me on both cheeks, "how are you Victor? I haven't seen you in here a whole lot lately. Business must be good for your too?"

"No complaints from me either," I said smiling, "other than I'm so hungry, I could eat a whole horse."

"Then let me get you a plate of my famous paella."

As he went off in the direction of the kitchen I shouted,

"With extra bread."

He threw his thumb in the air to signify he'd got it.

I turned and set my back to the bar and surveyed the room. The patrons were now being seated by Mei-Li's efficient team and in the far corner past the many uniformed personnel, I saw John Smith sitting alone, sporting as ever one of his neverending aray of bow ties. This one was green with pink spots. If Ginny was correct and he'd lost one of his men earlier today, he looked nothing like a man in mourning. Carlos returned and mixed me a good scotch with a little water, then found me a table near the back and told me my food would be out directly.

The food was always good and there was plenty of it but they cooked just the one thing each night, even for Carlos who benefited from knowing Percy, ingedients were scarce. Basically, if you were hungy enough, you'd eat what they had.

Mei-Li brought out my mountain of food and three door stops of cut bread, slathered in butter.

"Chew it sixty times doll," she whispered in my ear.

"Of course."

"And remember to breathe between mouthfuls."

I would have added, I do the jokes, but I was too busy stuffing my face.

My dad strolled in with Jimmy who made a beeline for Gloria, and whispered something in her ear. She laughed, looked across at me and faked shock by putting her hand up to her mouth. If she hadn't known earlier, she did now. Jimmy joined us and he and my dad ordered themselves a beer and plate of food as I was finishing up.

"How is sleeping beauty?"

"Just fine, Paul is with him. He woke up, and I made him eat something and drink a few cups of tea. Three hours later he couldn't keep his eyes open and I just about walked him back to his bed. He's asleep again and looks more comfortable this time."

Their drinks arrived with a kiss for each of us from Gloria, who whispered to me,

"I hear the cat's out of the bag."

To which I replied,

"He's punching well above his weight kid."

She kissed me again and went back to work.

"How come you got two?" Jimmy asked feigning jealousy.

"Animal magnatism, pure and simple."

The White Oyster's resident vocalist,Vonda Newton, was belting out a heart wrenching rendition of, 'The Man I Love' as her opening number and you could hear a pin drop, as all those seated were captivated by her version of the ballad. As the song ended, it was Gloria's chance to blow Jimmy a kiss. I did the same and was assualted with his homburg for my trouble.

We were a few drinks in when during the interval, John Smith stopped at our table, on his way to sample the indoor plumbing. He dropped into the empy seat and before he spoke I couldn't resist getting in the first barb,

"I understand you lost a man today?"

"You know I can't discuss operational issues with you Vic."

"I thought he was attending an auction?

He looked angry for just a second, but he quickly recovered his composure. Then what he said surprised me.

"Your friend is playing a dangerous game Vic."

"I assume you're referring to Agatha?"

"We both know who I'm talking about."

"Have it your way but know this, she isn't my friend. She dated my genuine friend over two years ago."

"Then why are you helping her?"

"For the same reason your man attended that auction I suspect."

"Oh by the way, I hear those two goons you butted heads with tonight gave Ginny the slip.

He got up and left smiling, leaving me shaking my head, the paella suddenly not sitting so well in my stomach.

At least I was now reasonably certain he didn't have Aggie, or the pieces she was selling. I just hoped Ginny and her men were unhurt.

"That gent always looks like he's trying to see seven different ways all at once," my dad quipped.

It tickled Jimmy and reminded me how insightful Charles Prince could be. It perfectly encapsulated the oh so slippery John Smith. It made me wonder whether Everton Cosgrove's newly found sensitivity, had something to do with my father's influence.

"Dad, you didn't by any chance try to persuade Everton to get in touch with his feelings?"

"It's good to feel son. Things that are bottled up can go bad."

I sat back and in my chair and smiled widely at him.

"I knew it. You know you just might have ruined a perfectly good psychopath."

"Vic don't be vulgar. Everton is a complex character. There's a reason he's the way he is."

I laughed hard.

"Maybe, but violence is his favourite meal."

"I don't dispute that, but he should feel something after he's eaten it."

The night went on like that, my father making sense of things in his inimitable way. I'd already made a mental note not to drink too much, so that I was sober enough, to keep an eye open for two rogue special forces operatives on my way home.

8

I was in my office finishing a cup of the good coffee, when two pairs of brogues came up my staircase fast. Thankfully they were moving much too quickly to be Sergeant Fitzpatrick and his sidekick. I hastily put my hand on the Webley pistol I'd recently installed in a holster, fixed under my desk, just in case Smith and Jones didn't get the message last night. I was relieved though, when in walked my two best friends, Percy and Jimmy. Percy looked like a new pin, in a chocolate brown pinstriped number and was even carrying an ivory walking cane, that matched the colour of his pristine, cream homburg. I slid the gun back where it belonged and kept my eyes off them, my face emotionless.

"I didn't realise the booze was affecting your balance so much."

Jimmy laughed and said,

"He thinks the prop makes him look distinguished Vic."

"He's always had more money than sense."

"Sure did, even when he was dirt poor."

"Erhum, I am here you know and I do have a heart murmer as you well know gentlemen."

"D'you hear something Jim?"

"I can just make out a few noises but it doesn't sound like an apology for the worry I put my friends through."

Percy crossed his arms and tried to frown but couldn't hold it for very long and was soon laughing with us. I made three more coffees and aked them whether this was just a social call.

"Look and before you both start, it isn't because you brought the subject up but yes I'm sorry for what I put everyone through. Especially your dad Vic. He doesn't need to be anybody's nurse maid right now."

"You're not wrong Percy," I said narrowing my eyes, "but what else do you want? You could have apologised over the blower."

"Anyone can pick up the phone and say they're sorry."

Not many in this city can in 1940 I thought, but instead I said, "come on spill it."

He put his hands up.

"I admit it. I still have feelings for the feline, there I said it and I know what you're going to say. She's no damn good. I know it, but knowing it doesn't help an awful lot."

It wasn't often I was stuck for words but this was one of those rare occasions.

Jimmy was equally silent.

"Do you think she shot those men?" Percy finally asked.

"My gut tells me no, but the truth is we don't have one clue what went on."

"She's stirring up a hornet's nest Vic," Percy went on.

"Right on," I added.

"I don't like it one bit," he continued, his expression suddenly grave.

"If she didn't know how valuable those items were when she first set foot in Liverpool, she'll know it now," Jimmy added.

I didn't add that I was convinced she'd always known the true worth of the pieces she was pedaling.

That's why she was convinced she could make a score, that would see her right for the rest of her days.

"We have to find her Vic. I can't sleep from the worry. I'm prepared to put as many bodies on this as it takes."

"What do you have in mind?" I asked.

"It was Jimmy's idea. He suggested flooding the city with men and I thought it might work, if I upped the anty by putting a price on her head, payable only if she's brought to me unharmed."

"Anything is worth a try, but you have to know that you're putting your ageing workforce up against professionals. You can do it either way but let me at least speak to Wilf before we go off half cocked."

"Sure Vic."

I put down my second coffee of the morning and called him at home and was told he was at the marina. I re-dialled his private number over there and got Ginny.

"I heard those two clowns are on the loose again. What happened?"

"Two cars full of gun toting heavies is what happened. They run us off the road, got the jump on us and just took them."

"Were you or your men hurt?"

"Only our pride sugar."

"Any idea who freed them?"

"None."

I explained about Percy's plan and Ginny thought anything was worth a try. I explained that we were planning to meet at Percy's brand new warehouse, over on Bramley Moore Dock, that afternoon. She said she'd alert Wilf and see if she couldn't persuade him to part with a few of his boys and that she'd come along herself. She also added that she was waiting to hear from a source, who knew a bit about Smith and Jones and their backgrounds.

*

We waited for Paul to pick us up and while we did, Jimmy went out for fish and chips. We were working on the assumption that it might be sometime until we ate again and it was closing on lunchtime. I'd have felt a little more confident with Everton in our ranks, but there was just the small matter of stopping him from permanently, putting out Agatha's lights, if we did actually locate her.

Jimmy returned with our food, wrapped in newsprint as was the custom and the smell of the salt and vinegar leaking into yesterday's papers was mouth watering. I looked across at Percy who couldn't wait to unwrap his and said,

"Should quieten down the snakes in your stomach eh Percy?"

He was too busy stuffing his face to answer and instead put a thumb up in my direction. I got Jimmy and I a plate but Percy wouldn't hear of it. Paul appeared a few minutes after we'd started to eat and thankfully his was still warm.

When we'd had our fill, we each used my solitary tap and washed the grease off our fingers, before dashing out to the car.

*

The warehouse was more like a giant underground bunker, buried under tons of concrete and I could immediately understand why on the drive over, Percy told us he might move his entire operation to the site. I didn't like to even speculate on how thick the floor and walls would have needed to be. The place was as dry as a bone when most places along the river bank were prone to flooding this time of year. Above it was a shelter for the workers, which indicated how deep it went and how bomb proof he thought it was. There must have been more than fifty of them waiting when we walked in, their ages ranging from mid-forties to anywhere up to late sixties. They were in groups of four and five in working men's clothing. Ordinarily they might be smoking, but Paul explained that Percy had a strict no smoking policy inside all of his storage facilities. Standing apart from them and looking more like a bookeeper than a trained killer stood Roderick Peters, a folded newspaper in one hand, a pencil in the other and a pair of hornrimmed spectacles on his face. He'd clearly been working on a crossword. I shook his hand and introduced him to Jimmy and Paul, as Percy gathered his men around him.

We listened from a distance, as he explained that he wanted them to speak to every contact they had in the city. Over half present were white, so there was no need to explain how rare it was in some parts of Merseyside for a black woman to show her face. The assumption being that someone must have noticed her. He was offering five hundred quid for her safe return and fifty to any man who brought back solid information, that led to her being located. Finally, he handed each man two five pound notes, but added that he wanted this to be used to grease the wheels for any additional work. He didn't want word going around that he was paying for information, as they didn't have the time to or the manpower to verify every potential sighting. He re-iterated it was dangerous and that no man was expected to get in the way of any trouble. If they were to pick up a tail, or sniff out an interested party, under no circumstances should they engage in any form of altercation. He explained that others on the lookout for Aggie were likely to be professionals and no amount of bravery would succeed against highly trained operatives.

He ended by inviting them to go and grab a cuppa and a bite to eat in the canteen, while they awaited further instructions. They drifted out to the sound of hushed voices. Leaving Percy free to join us. I introduced him to Roderick and they shook hands.

"I heard a bit about what you did for Vic up in Southport a few months ago and we're all grateful. As far as Vic is concerned, you're the best there is at what you do, so we're really pleased to have your help," he said, then looked at his watch and turned back to Roderick once again, "I don't suppose you've any idea when Ginny might be arriving?"

"She should be here now. Something must have come up."

"Is she coming alone?"

"Not to my knowledge," he said, excused himself, then looked across at me, "I heard something that might be of interest to you Vic."

"Go on."

"I have on good authority that your old nemesis Sergeant Fitzpatrick is moonlighting for John Smith."

I uttered a dry sardonic laugh,

"It explains his interest in Aggie's activities but I shouldn't be surprised. He'd sell his mother down the river for beer money."

Before we could utter another word, in walked Wilf, Ginny and four men in their wake. I recognised them all. The two older men were colleagues of Roderick's. Men who'd retired before the war but had signed up to help the war effort on home soil. Peter Abbot was tall with a loping gait and Max Zingel, squat and swarthy. I'd encountered them at the home of an Italian with mob connections and fascist sympathies, when I was working in Southport during early summer. The two younger men, probably in their forties, I'd seen at Wilf's place recently. One was a giant of a man, tall and wide enough to block out the sun and I heard them call him Alec. The other I'd heard called Jim. He had a similar build to Peter Abbot but was even thinner even though he was about an inch shorter. He may well have been mute for all I knew, because I'd never actually heard him speak.

Before they reached us, Percy was told there was a call for him in the office.

Wilf looked tired.

"You okay?" I asked.

"I've had better days Vic."

"Anything you want to share?"

"Not unless you're my priest."

"Speak slowly my son," I quipped and that almost got a smile out of him.

"I have something to talk about as long as you're still taking confessions Father Prince," Ginny said.

"Unburden yourself my child," I continued on.

"Get this, Smith, Jones and Afia were all in the service together. They were commandos and chosen for a special detail."

"Just the three of them?"

"Four in total honeypie, one of their number a fella called Jamie Cole, didn't make it. Don't know the specifics I'm afraid, but can you guess who they were ordered to protect?"

I wet my lips and resisted the urge to whistle a happy tune.

"Seamus Long?"

Long was the man who had manufactured the *Nine Lives*. Our paths crossed in late summer.

"Close but no cigar."

"Come on Ginny put me out of my misery."

"Herbert O'Brien."

"Of course, your ex-husband."

"How droll."

I was referring to our first meeting in the Spring when Ginny, then gainfully employed by the US Government and a certain John Smith, who'd persuaded her to present herself to me as the widow of O'Brien. That was until she was shot full of holes, in a bungled attempt to storm a fortified residence.

"You ain't heard the best of it yet sugar. Their names are actually Henry Smith and Walter Jones."

I shook my head.

"Any way of tying them to Aggie?"

"Nothing official but wasn't she meeting Afia in Thornton?"

"They were all there at the same time, but a meeting is stretching our knowledge just a little."

Percy walked back into the large unit, his steps brisk and business like and before Ginny could argue her theory any further, his expression brought all talk to an abrupt end.

“I’ve had a man watching her Dad’s place. She was spotted there twenty minutes ago, going inside.”

“How do you see this going?” Wilf asked. He was good. We all knew he’d brought the firepower and the expertise but he was still prepared to give deference to Percy, who after all, had arranged this little party.

“I’ve told none of my men about this. If she’s been spotted by us there’s a chance others have her on their radar,” he said and I could see this was a massive effort for him. I’d only ever seen an expression on his face like this once before. The day she left him. He went on, “the way I see it, if there’s gun play we can handle it. As willing as my men are, they’d only get in the way. So I’ll send them on their merry way on their errands and I say we go in nice and quiet, scope the place out, put a ring around it. Then I just walk up to her dad’s place as casually as you like.”

“We,” I said.

“What?”

“We, meaning you and me, walk up to her old man’s front door.”

He smiled for the first time since we’d entered the warehouse. Removing his homberg, he fanned himself with it and I could see the sweat beaded in his hairline.

“Okay Vic you win, on the basis that you’ll probably shoot me in the foot if I try to go in alone.”

“Damn right.”

“Okay then Wyart Earp and Doc Holiday, why don’t we mosey on over there, before she hi-tails it?” Ginny added, in her broadest southern drawl.

*

We took the short drive to the holy land, as it was known locally, because of several streets named after the prophets. Agatha's father lived bang in the centre of Moses street, the end of four adjoined properties. We positioned our vehicles at each end of the long road, made up of a mix of Victorian semi detached and terraced houses, leaving the back entries as the only way out on foot.

The street was nice and peaceful, maybe a little too quiet. There were no children playing which was unsual and as I climbed out of the car, the hairs on the back of my neck stood on end.

"Looks serene Vic."

"Knock it off Percy, there isn't a stray dog or cat about and I haven't heard a single chorus of bird song."

"We are in the Dingle Vic, a concrete jungle, duh."

I leaned in and whispered,

"Trust me on this, we aren't the only casual visitors in the holy land today."

"Shit. What do we do now then?"

"Stick to the plan."

"We'll be sitting ducks."

"I thought you might have realised that, when you made your big speech back in the warehouse."

He had a look on his face that I couldn't read.

"Come on Percy, we have a team of crack shots covering our backs."

"It's no good if my back's full of holes."

"Then I'll go in alone."

"Oh, no you don't."

Ginny coughed and yelled, "are you two cowboys ever going into the OK Coral any time soon? I'm freezing my ass off out here."

Wilf who was closeby stepped toward us, light on his feet, despite his brooding look and those dark circles under his eyes, that must have been weighing him down.

"This is your show Percy but if you're having second thoughts we can do this differently. We can just put our heads together and come up with an alternative plan."

"Vic thinks we have company."

"Oh they're here alright. So what's it to be?"

Percy swallowed hard, straightened his tie, repositioned his hat, then looked Wilf in the eye and said,

"We're going in."

We strolled down Moses street like we had a hundred times before, when we were just kids, but we were fooling nobody. I felt eyes on us and just hoped they wanted to know what a knock on a certain door might reveal, before emptying their weapons into two easy targets.

We approached the door and I spread my hands, as Percy put his hand on his piece. His chest was rising and falling like the pistons on an express train. I took a deep breath and gave the knocker a good rap. The echo along the empty street sounded like the church bell for morning mass. The door opened inward and I saw the barrel of the browning pistol, before my eyes captured the grinning face of Henry Smith. I went back on my haunches so that I could generate some power and kicked the door into his body, with the soul of my shoe. The force sent the door catapaulting into him and the firearm fell to the threadbare carpet. I grabbed Percy, spun him around and told him to run. I knew he could outrun me when were kids, but I hadn't counted on him still possessing such speed. I just about stayed with him, long enough to knock him to the ground as bullets began to rain over our sprawled bodies.

Jim and Alec approached us as their colleagues fired back in unison. Alec picked me up like I was a feather duster and carried me beyond our corden of cars, where Paul and Jimmy stood together. Jim the mute followed just behind him and dumped Percy beside me.

"They're shooting from another place across the street too," Jimmy said.

Wilf looked across at a house that had been rendered and painted a peculiar, racing green colour. There looked to a shooter at both the lower front and upper windows. At the other end of the street, Ginny, Roderick, Max and Peter spotted Wilf's gestures and they began to return fire to the other house.

Percy was dusting himself down behind the cover of one of the cars. He looked up at me and said,

"This is actually like gunfight at the OK coral."

Wilf joined us as Jim and Alec started to return fire.

"We're thinking of going in the back way of her dad's place," he said looking at Percy.

"Wilf this is your party now. I'm all out of ideas and bravery."

"We don't have enough men to put a ring around the entire street, so I suppose what I'm saying is, whoever is shooting from the green house could escape without us ever knowing who they are."

I shrugged my shoulders and reluctantly took the Webley sidearm Wilf was offering me and turned to face my friends.

"Percy, Paul, stay here in case any of them make a break for it this way."

They nodded in agreement as Percy pulled an extra gun out of the car and handed it to Paul. He looked at it as if he'd never seen one in his life. I looked up toward the other end of the street and saw that Peter and Max had stayed with the other cars.

"Come on Vic," Wilf said and Jimmy and I followed him, Alec and Jim into the back entry, we had to step carefully as it was littered with garbarge and evidence of canine activity. When we got to the rear of the property, we met Ginny and Roderick, who were already in place, peering around the open gate into a small back yard.

"Anything?" Wilf asked.

"Not a peep. The gate was open when we got here" Ginny answered.

I pushed past them and walked into the square shaped yard, thinking if her father was tooled up, he might not hesitate before shooting. I saw a face I recognised through the back kitchen window and she beckoned me in. I stepped through the door, my gun still out in front of me.

"How are things Aunt Alice?" I asked in a hushed voice.

"Those two white boys ran upstairs when George pulled out his old service revolver and started shooting."

She looked terrified.

"Agatha?"

She just shook her thin face, whatever that meant. Before I could question her, a couple more shots came from inside the house.

"Alice go and wait outside with my friends, while we find out what's going on up there."

Ginny and Roderick stepped inside, as Wilf was resting his own jacket on the shoulders of Aggie's aunt. Jim and Alec were still in the alley keeping watch and Jimmy remained with Wilf, after I gestured for him to stay where he was. I went into the narrow hallway and could smell the cordite from the shots that had already been fired. I got to the bottom of the stairs and looked up, but saw nothing in the strange monochrome light.

"George, if you're up there this is Vic Prince."

I thought I heard footsteps and a door open before a famliar voice responded, sounding breathless.

"I hope that crooked friend of yours isn't with you, because he's not welcome."

George never thought Percy was good enough for Agatha.

"You okay, not wounded?"

"I'm okay boy but if those two clowns show their ugly mugs again they won't be."

"Where are they?"

"I chased them up into the roofspace."

I turned to face Ginny and Roderick, who urged me to go up and as I did they followed. We moved cautiously up the creaking staircase and when I reached the top, George peeked out from the back bedroom. The loft hatch was hinged and hung open. Beneath it stood a tall step ladder in the shape of a giant letter 'A' that was splattered with paint.

"They dragged that thing out of this room while I was doing my best to get up here after them. My chest isn't what it was and it slows me down, but I got a couple of shots off as they went in."

We stopped and listened but could hear nothing.

"I'm going to take a look," I said.

"Hold on, they could be just waiting for someody to poke their head in," Ginny piped up.

"There's only one way to find out."

I gingerly stepped onto the wooden ladder that swayed slightly and creaked from my weight.

"It'll hold son,"George assured me, "I reckon I'm at least two stone heavier than you and it supports my weight."

Standing on the top rung, I was just tall enough to take a squint. Before I extended to my full height Ginny pressed her cigarette lighter into my hand. I almost dropped it as I lost my balance for moment, while extending. I held my breath as I thrust my large head into the space, before pulling my arm in and flicking the lighter on. I wasn't surprised to see a big fat nothing. The loft space was a large rectangular area that ran across all four adjoining houses. I thought I could see a light from another open hatch at the far end. I ducked my head back in to explain what I'd seen .

"Then they've given us the slip," Ginny said.

"I'll alert Wilf," Roderick added before putting his piece away and descending the stairs.

"Do I go in after them?" I asked Ginny.

She shook her head.

"I'd say we put a man up there though, just in case they're cornered in the end house but my instinct says they're long gone."

"We've got the back and the front covered."

"I hope you're right."

Jim the mute came up the stairs as I descended the ladder and Ginny asked him to go up and wait. He nodded and did as instructed. George had come out of the bedroom, his smoking pistol still in his hand. He was wearing a ratty old grey dressing gown and hadn't shaved for a couple of days. His chest sounded like his lungs were full of tiny holes. It must have been over three years since I'd seen him and then he was an imposing figure, still brimming with vitality, but whatever ailed him had taken it's toll.

"Where is she George?"

"Well out of your interfering clutches by now I hope."

"Believe it or not, we came here to help."

"By stopping her selling her treasures?"

"Her treasures? What do you know about it?"

"Enough to know that when the deal is done, she's taking me away from this filthy city. Somewhere I can get good clean air back into my lungs."

"Wake up George, the world is at war, where will you go?"

"You let me worry about that."

Roderick came back up the stairs and looked at Ginny and I.

"She's hiding in the cellar."

"My sister's always had a big mouth," Agatha's father added, wearing a sour expression. I shook my head and made my way downstairs.

He shuffled forward and shouted after us,

"I want you out of my house."

We ignored him and approached Wilf and Aunt Alice, who were stood at the open door to the cellar, peering into the darkness.

I nodded and told them I'd go and bring her up. I flicked on Ginny's lighter again and descended the uneven stairs into a dusty, damp smelling area that covered the square area of the house. I walked cautiously calling out her name. I eventually found my way to a wall that butted up to the back yard and a small window that only looked big enough for a twelve year old to get through. It flapped open like a gaping mouth, telling us how stupid we'd been. I turned back and climbed up to deliver the bad news, as George eventually joined us, his chest wheezing. He was breathing as though he'd been on a five mile hike and when he spoke his voice was small and brittle, as though it was an incredible effort to utter a simple sentence. He was was smiling though, as his words that were meant to mock us, only made me feel maudlin,

"I taught my girl to scrap, shoot and think just as good as any man. The truth is you've all met your match and I bet it hurts just like the pain in my chest."

9

That night most of us drowned our sorrows at the White Oyster club. Percy informed us he was still tired and the last thing he needed was any more alcohol. I suspected that was only partly true. The other reason was his concern for Agatha's safety and the disappointment of getting so close to keeping her safe, at least from his perspective. I also felt he was reluctant to show us a face riddled with worry.

I was well into my second scotch and water when in walked my dad and Paul, as Vonda was finishing a perfect rendition of Hoagy Carmichael's, Stardust.

My father smiled and clapped as Paul was ordering them a drink.

"I always liked that song son."

"Pity you missed most of it."

"If you think that, perhaps you're not quite the detective you think you are?"

I smiled.

"We were watching from the back and thought we'd enjoy it without disturbing the room."

"Sure you did dad. I told Paul, eight. You two'd be late for your own funerals."

"I hope so. Anyhow if you don't believe me ask Everton."

"Everton?"

"Now I know you are making it up. Mr Cosgrove is currently recuperating in a plush nursing home, somewhere in Formby."

He raised a quizzical eyebrow.

"There's nothing wrong with my eyesight boy, look for yourself."

He pointed to the bar before he and Paul took their seats, just as their beers arrived.

I turned my gaze to the crowded bar and nearly fell out of my chair. Chatting to Jimmy, in one of his customary pinstriped suits, stood the one and only, Everton Cosgrove. The suit was black, with broad white stripes and looked new, perhaps his Sunday best. A white silk hanky in his top pocket was almost as rare as the wide smile on his face. On his arm was an eye catching woman, a couple of inches shorter than he, with an hourglass figure. She looked as though she'd got into her skin tight black dress with the aid of a hot spoon. I started to get up to find out how on earth he'd escaped back to the city, when Paul piped up,

"You're liable to catch flies with your mouth open that way son,"

I picked my hat up and swiped him with it, on my way to where Everton and his lady friend stood holding court.

I stared at him side on but he didn't flinch.

"Does Wilf know you're AWOL?"

"Victor, allow me to introduce you to Kaya."

"Charmed," I said.

"We colonists should stick together, isn't that right Kaya?"

"Absolutely Mr Cosgrove, Kingston and Capetown are as one."

Hers was a cultured South African voice, whereas Everton's Jamican lilt was quite pronounced even though as I understood it, he left the place when he he was a mere child.

He turned to me as Jimmy and Kaya ordered themselves a gimlet each and another dark rum and blackcurrent for Everton, from one of the shark-like waitresses, who were perpetually moving.

"You probably heard that I got friendly with a nurse up in the sticks and when I heard she was coming to the city for a few days, I decided I'd had enough of that place."

"How was it?"

"It was a just fine but it isn't right to waste anymore of Percy's money. That stuff is well and truly out of my system."

"Well he'll thank you for that."

"How is he?"

"Worried."

"About that damn fool woman."

Everton raised his eyes to the ceiling.

"And he'll be more concerned when he learns that you're on the loose."

"Forget what I said back in Hoylake. That was only my pride talking."

I narrowed my eyes.

"So you're saying if Aggie walked in here now, you wouldn't try to put her lights out?"

"I'm not saying I wouldn't want to."

I shook my head.

"The Everton Cosgrove I know is primed to act on certain impulses."

"A man can change Vic. You should ask your old man, he talks a lot of sense."

I smiled.

"I know you too have spoken but just so that we've got this crystal clear, you've no longer got a hard for killing Percy's ex?"

"Correct," he said, before sliding his arm around around the waist of his date and picking up his drink.

They then wondered off and found a table, leaving Jimmy and I alone.

I leaned in and said,

“I wouldn’t let Everton catch you looking at his woman that way.”

“It isn’t him I’ve got to worry about.”

Right on cue Gloria slapped his backside on her way past, turning to wink at his smiling face.

“I take your point.”

I got myself another drink and on my way back to my table Jimmy called me over.

“What’s up?”

“How are you going to keep Everton from joining in on our resumption of the search for Agatha tomorrow?”

“Maybe we don’t need to?”

“Hold on, I thought he’d swore he’d kill her.”

“He says he’d still like to, but now realises it was an over reaction.”

“He said that?”

“Well not in those exact words, but you get the idea.”

“Will Percy buy it?”

“If he doesn’t then I suppose he won’t be tagging along. After all, Percy funds his rent and what he puts in his mouth. There aren’t too many well paid jobs growing on trees in these parts, whether we’re at war or not.”

*

Next day I was up early.

It was Percy's idea to check out all the places he and Aggie frequented when they were a couple. He'd clearly had time to think and change his strategy. Instead of flooding the city with bodies, he thought he might find her in familiar surroundings and I liked this idea better. Not only did it have a little more finesse, I thought it had some credence. She'd been out of the city for years and after all, who did she know other than her family or friends? As we were her only friends, that I knew of, I took the view she'd be expecting us to keep tabs on her family, which we did with Wilf's help. So, it stood to reason to me at least, that she might almost hide in plain sight. Somewhere her black face wasn't such a rarity and that's why Percy's new idea made lots of sense to me.

Paul picked me up bright and early at my place. I left Mei-Li sleeping and stepped into one of those dry autumn days that was cold in the shade, but had plenty of sunshine to warm your face. I was finishing a slab of dry bread as the car pulled up and with no time to grab a drink, I hoped we might grab a cuppa somewhere along our route. They pulled to the curb in a common and garden Morris 8, hoping to blend in, rather than use the rather ostentatious white Rolls. Percy was seated upfront alongside him. I pushed my head inside first and said,

"Ready for that cup of cha whenever you're ready to stop."

As I squeezed my big frame into the less than roomy rear, Percy shook his head.

"Christ Vic haven't you had breakfast?"

"Sorry if I don't yet live in the lap of luxury, like a certain black marketeer. I had to tip toe around while Mei-Li was sleeping."

Paul chuckled.

"I'd pay to see that," he added.

"If you'd woken her Vic, she was liable to give you a shiner," Percy went on laughing.

Once they'd had their morning mirth at my expense, we set off, destination unknown.

It was all in Percy's head.

"Is it just us?"

"No Ginny is picking up Jimmy and Everton and meeting us at Sefton Park."

"So, you're happy with him tagging along?"

"We had a long talk. He knows what she means to me."

I caught Paul's eyes in the rear view and they looked as unsure as I was about it.

"Besides if he harms her, I'll kill him myself."

I didn't doubt he'd try, but I could never see him pulling it off.

The green, wide-open spaces of the large Park always brought a smile to my face. From the day I could walk unaided, my father and I could be found here come rain or shine, on any day he didn't have to work. For families who only had cramped two up, two down homes and a small yard, like us, the parks were a godsend. We enjoyed exercise, clean air and through my father's tutelage, I developed a love of nature.

We parked and Paul and Percy lit up a smoke, while we waited for the others to arrive.

"We used to climb trees and kick a ball around here when we were kids, but I never knew you and Agatha came to the park."

Percy smiled and a dreamy expression flowered on his face.

"Are you kidding Vic, we were always out on the boating lake. Aggie loved being on the water. She'd trail her long figures in the water on warm summer days. There was only one problem when I was rowing."

"What was that?"

"She used to tease me about my technique. Hell, we both knew she was better at it than me."

Paul creased up at that and almost swallowed his smoke.

"I bet she was Percy," I said, as Ginny pulled up in Wilf's mark IV Jaguar. The long bonnet was a highly polished burgundy and the side panels the same colour split with cream. She, Jimmy and Everton climbed out.

"I could get used to traveling like this Vic," Jimmy quipped.

I nodded to the other two. Ginny looked at Percy and said,

"Ready to be deployed sir."

Percy smiled before answering.

"Can I suggest that someone checks Lark Lane and the rest of us cover the park? Meet back her in one hour."

"If we find her, then what?" Paul asked.

"Bring her back here."

"What if she won't come?" Jimmy asked.

"Try to persuade her."

"She might be armed."

"She will be packing Jim, that's for sure."

Ginny put her hand up.

"Yes?" Percy asked.

"Can I suggest we use these if she won't come back with us?"

She pulled four whistles out of her bag.

"They're pretty good and their sound carries quite well. If we spot her, blow it long and hard and keep doing that until we find you."

"Sounds like a plan," Percy said.

Jimmy took the first whistle.

"I'll take the Lark Lane detail."

"Lovers lane, eh Jim?"

"Stop it Vic, we're not twelve anymore," he said, but he was grinning like he still might be.

"That leaves five of us and three whistles," I said.

Ginny threw one to me, but before she could say anything Percy piped up.

"You're a big boy Vic you can go it alone, Everton and I will take a stroll towards the boating lake"

"I guess that leaves Paul and I," Ginny said, "I think I got lucky."

"I think we both did," Paul said in agreement.

I volunteered to walk the perimeter of the park, heading west as far as the beautiful Victorian palm house. Ginny and Paul went through the centre as Percy and Everton headed east. It was still a fine, dry day, considering all of the poor weather we'd had so far in early Autumn, but I decided it might be wise to stay off the grass. It was too early for most people and as I strolled off on my own, I marvelled as I always did, at the sound of the birdsong and the beauty that was all around us. Nature had a way of pushing on, no matter what obstacles humanity continued to put in its way.

Forty-five minutes later, I'd made it back to the car without a siting of Agatha. The complete circumference is around two and a half miles and we felt we pretty much covered it all. Jimmy was waiting for us with two flasks.

"No joy?" he asked as I arrived back first.

"I see you got lucky though."

"Madge who manages the tea-room has taken a shine to Gloria and me."

"You make such a sweet couple after all."

"Another crack like that and I'm liable to take my false leg off and start clouting you with."

I laughed hard.

"Don't do that, just poor me a cuppa, I'm spitting feathers."

The hot, sweet tea hit the back of my dry throat and went down a treat. I was on my second cup when Ginny and Paul strolled into view, shaking their heads, closely followed by Percy and Everton. As Jimmy passed the tea around, he explained how he'd come to acquire two flasks of hot liquid. I looked across at Percy as a light bulb come on over his head. He spontaneously uttered the word,

"Mickie's"

Everyone stopped talking and turned to face him.

"I think I know where she is. This tearoom is your place, you and Gloria I mean, Jim. Mickie's was ours."

"Mickie's fish shack on the dock road?" Paul asked.

"The very place," Percy said, a beaming smile on his face.

"Isn't that up near the new warehouse?"

"Pretty much," he said, that dreamy look on his face again, "she loved the food and the water lapping against the pilings after dark."

"After dark?" I said.

"Mickie rents out a couple of very nice rooms. We'd often stay the night."

"Are you thinking she's been there all along, right under our noses."

"Maybe."

*

We returned the flasks to Madge on the way to Mickie's and on the way over, Percy explained how fresh and tasty the food was. It got so I could practically taste the chowder, he described it in such sumptuous detail.

We parked the cars in a side street and walked across to a rectangular building, painted a fading, sky blue, so that it had a deliberate, weathered look. Adjacent to it was a row of bench seats and a section of railing looking out onto the lively river, feeding into the Atlantic. I saw the feline right away. She had her back to us but her fine figure stood out, as she looked out onto the waters of the Mersey, seemingly without a care in the world. I held everyone back and let Percy approach alone. He nonchalantly strolled to her side and eased his arm around her narrow waist. It was a tender moment, between two people who'd been inseparable for a couple of years and I believed they deserved some privacy, so much so, that I felt like a voyeur, observing my friend and the girl who had been the moon and stars to him and probably still was. They held each other and kissed passionately. As I looked on, I knew that despite all she'd told me on that first night we'd become reacquainted, she still had feelings for him. So, what had this wild goose chase all this about, pride? A determination to set her only course in life. I didn't have the answer.

*

We waited until Percy gave us the nod. When he did, we strolled over *en masse*. I was watching Everton but as usual his expression was hard to read. Percy offered to buy us all an early lunch. As we sat, I found myself beside Ginny and couldn't help myself,

"I guess this is what you and Wilf call brunch?"

She went to elbow me in the ribs and I caught her sharp bone in my palm.

I was disappointed there was no chowder on the menu, but instead I ordered a bowl of the special, which was Mickie's salt fish stew. It was excellent. Only Agatha and Paul had a bite with me. Both opting for a slice of home-made apple pie. It seemed that Agatha had been staying at Mickie's after all and she disclosed to Percy there were a few things she wanted to discuss with him alone. We got the message, but as I got up to leave, he leaned across and whispered something. He wanted me to ask my father to cook up one of his famous pans of scouse. I knew his housekeeper, Millie, was a good baker but cooking wasn't her speciality. Then he said a little louder;

"Let's say we all meet at my place at 5. I'll bring Agatha with me."

I nodded and left him speaking to Paul, who listened to his employer, then strolled over to where we stood near the exit, most of our group smoking.

"He wants me to pick him up just after half past four. Can I drop you, Jimmy and Everton somewhere?"

Before we could answer, Ginny turned her back to Percy and Agatha and asked,

"What's to stop her giving him the slip?"

"Nothing I suppose,"

"Then why are we leaving?"

"I could hang around and keep an eye out for Percy," Everton said.

I didn't think that was a good idea. All it took was Agatha attempting to give Percy the slip and getting herself accidently shot by him.

"You stand out like a sore thumb, in fact we all would. Can Wilf spare anyone to keep an eye on them?"

She tapped her lips with her spare index finger, narrowed her eyes, then as she ground out her cigarette butt under her shoe, she nodded and said,

"I have an idea that might work."

I found out much later that Bill who worked at the marina, a man who skippered us from Wilf's home, to the safe house, aboard the *Windjammer,* what seemed like an age ago, had taken a smaller vessel up the Mersey estuary and anchored it directly in line with Mickie's. There he watched Percy and Agatha with the aid of binoculars, and a radio handy, in the event she did actually attempt to disappear again.

It was a waste of manpower as it turned out, when they both arrived at Percy's, looking windswept and happy to be away from the coast and a stiff wind that had blown inland, and seemingly like the feline herself, coming up out of nowhere.

*

Mei-li joined us as it was one of her nights off. Jimmy ate with us but planned to depart for *The White Oyster* club at some point, to be near a certain Gloria Potter. My father and Paul did the cooking and even Ginny and Wilf tagged along. Everton had another date with Kaya, so we left him to it. The further apart he and Agatha where suited me.

The food was excellent. Known locally as blind scouse, the dish was essentially a stew devoid of meat. Proving that even the city's most effective black marketeer, sometimes struggled to get hold of certain provisions. My dad had always been a bit of culinary wizard. I tasted celery and tabasco in the sauce and even had a second helping, as most of my fellow diners lit up a smoke. Percy brewed some of the good coffee and we all had a decent cup of java. The conversation was light and easy and if anybody had walked in on us, seated about Percy's oak dining room table, they would never have guessed that we were about to discuss the most sought after prize of the war effort, to date. We were just like a group of old friends catching up. Me-Li always liked Agatha and I could see they were happy to be in each other's company again. They hugged initially and when we were eating, Percy seated Aggie next to him and Mei-Li took it upon herself to sit directly opposite.

When the coffee cups had been drained, my dad and Paul excused themselves to do the washing up and when I objected, thinking they'd done enough, they told me they insisted. Paul said they'd each had enough of the *Nine Lives* to last them a lifetime. He said the dishes were getting a cat's lick, then they were off home to sit in front of the fire and listen to the wireless. Mei-Li asked me if it was appropriate for her to stay in the room and I put my big hand on hers and smiled, telling her she was only going to learn what every crook and spook in the city already knew.

Jimmy wanted to freshen up before his walk to the club, so excused himself, leaving six of us. We were honoured to be invited into the large back parlour, where there were six comfortable armchairs. The room had been another place he and Aggie used to spend a lot of time together and if I was right, I think she picked out the furniture, carpets, wallpaper and even the original art on the walls. The only thing that would have changed since her last visit, was the blackout curtains.

As she stepped across the threshold she paused and said,

"It's exactly as I remember it,"

It might have been a trick of the light but I was certain her eyes moistened, seeing the place again.

We found ourselves a seat and Percy put a drink in everyone's hand. Only then did Wilf bring up the elephant in the room.

"Agatha, I've been authorised by Mr Churchill himself, to furnish you with ten percent more than your best offer for those pieces you have."

She put her gimlet down and the look on her face could only be described as astonishment.

"But you don't even know what I've been promised for them."

"We don't care. We need to secure them. If they fall into enemy hands, we might never turn this damn war around."

It was a sobering thought.

"I'm not accepting their value in *War Bonds* either," she quipped, then the smile on her face quickly vaporised as she paused, seemingly searching for the right words, "there is just one tiny problem," she added, before taking a slug from her crystal tumbler.

"Go on," Wilf responded, his face expressionless.

"I met with a representative of my potential buyer, who took one of the items away to authenticate it."

Wilf's expression suddenly looked tight and he sat back in his chair. It was clearly a hammer blow and I was sure that after finding her and making his pitch, her words had taken the wind out of his sails.

I sat forward.

"Is there another meet set up?"

"I'm waiting for a note to arrive at Mickie's."

I nodded, took a sip of my scotch and narrowed my eyes.

"So, if they agree to buy, what was your next play?"

She locked eyes with mine and I briefly got a sense of what was driving her. A kind of steely determination, that had almost seen her turn her back on all of us.

"I was planning to fix it so that the switch was on my terms."

Percy was already on his third brandy and was becoming a little more tactile, and as he interlaced his fingers with hers, he said,

"That's one smart move."

"What if we lured them to a location we could control," Wilf then asked, "would that work for you?"

"I get it. We've got to get that piece back if I'm going to hand them all over. I don't have any problem with that at all."

"Good, then as soon as you hear from them, alert me through Percy or Vic, and we'll set it up."

"What if other factions get wind of the meeting?" Percy asked.

"They probably will, that's one of the reasons I'd rather it took place at a location that's works for us. That way we can be ready for them."

After that the conversation lightened, as though a weight had been lifted from the atmosphere. This was followed by laughter as the alcohol continued to flow. That was until Mei-Li innocently asked a question, four of us had wondered about, from the day the feline returned to Liverpool with her cargo.

"How did you get your mitts on those things?"

She was talking about the *Nine Lives* and suddenly all eyes turned back to Agatha.

"I was in Ireland, running a small country hotel in County Cork, when I was introduced to Horatio Afia, by a man who bet that I could out do him in a shooting contest. They set it up and guess what?"

"You beat him without even trying too hard," I added.

She smiled and saluted me.

"Was it clay pigeon?"

"No, good old-fashioned targets at 50 yards. He took it well though and we became friends, only friends," she said, looking across at Percy, "he had a wife he constantly talked about. Anyway, one night when he was pissed up in the bar, he let slip that him and his friends had acquired something that was going to make them very rich men, but he was worried they were going to cut him out of the deal. Next morning, we played a round of golf."

"Which you also won?" Percy asked.

"Of course. To be fair, H wasn't much of player, with ball and stick. During the game though, I persuaded him to let me hold them for him in return for a small cut. That's another reason why I came back home. I got them out of Ireland, while his two comrades watched him around the clock. He was the one who came up with the idea of running the auction, which I never thought was a good idea and it turned out it got him killed."

"Who punched his clock?" I asked.

"I heard it was a bloke he only referred to as Smith," she said and after she said his name, it was as if her mouth was suddenly filled with poison.

"You're talking about Henry, not John."

A puzzled look crossed her face.

"Who's John Smith."

I explained, doing my best to keep my language out of the gutter.

"I heard they took the pieces from Herbert O'Brien," Wilf said.

Aggie shrugged her shoulders as if she'd never heard of him.

"He was found dead in his munitions factory and on the death certificate, it says heart attack, but it was as the result of imbibing a dangerous barbiturate."

The room suddenly went quiet and Agatha frowned, but her expression gave nothing else away.

"He was killed with *Veronal*. That shit you put in Everton's coffee," Ginny said and she almost spat the words out and looked just as angry as she was that morning in Hoylake, when she found Everton and Toby unconscious in the safe house.

Aggie put her hands up.

"Hey this is getting out of hand Ginny; I didn't invite you here to start accusing people of things they didn't do."

"How do you know?"

"How do I know what?"

"How do you know she didn't kill O'Brien?"

"Stop it both of you. I swiped that stuff from Afia," Agatha said.

"So, you're blaming a dead man who can't speak up for himself. I hate to break this to you sugar, but I'm struggling to believe a single word that comes out of your mouth. Everton and Toby were both given about the right dose. How come, was that just a wild guess?"

Wilf put his hand on Ginny's arm as she reached for her drink and when he spoke, his words were more conciliatory.

"Do you know what happened to the fifth piece?"

"The what?"

"There are five pieces unaccounted for and you're only carrying four."

She smiled for the first time in what seemed like an age.

"Well three actually. No Wilf, I don't know anything about those pieces. And to make this absolutely clear, the *Veronal* was in an overnight bag with the *Nine Lives*, and I say this on my father's life," she went on, then crossed herself, before looking up at Ginny with a venom in her eyes, "also, my old man was pharmacist when he could work. I showed him the stuff and he explained the exact dose required."

Percy nodded and said, “that part is true.”

Ginny still didn’t like it but held her tongue and I didn’t blame her. That stuff was outlawed because it killed people.

“One final question, I promise,” Wilf said, “where are they now?”

Agatha’s face transformed from frown, into a devious grin.

My guess was she’d never reveal where they were, but I was dead wrong.

She kicked off her shoes, flipped them over and whacked each one heavily on the carpet. They’d clearly been custom made and the inner shoe hollowed out. In the right shoe were two miniature cats, in the left, the remaining piece. We all marvelled at them, so small and so delicately crafted, in three classic cat poses. Like I did when I first gazed at the four I’d acquired, I asked myself the inevitable question. What secret did they hold that made them so valuable?

“I had them made so that I could hide my money and jewellery. I won’t lie, I’ve mixed with some unsavoury types to try and make a score.”

Wilf wrapped things up by explaining he’d come up with a plan and a location for the meeting and would wait for the word. Ginny and he left and when they did, a tension left the room. Clearly Ginny and Aggie were never going to be friends and as soon as they departed, it was almost like the old days again, just Percy and I, and our girls, chatting, laughing and drinking. It sure took me back. I looked across at my friend, who looked a couple of drinks from tipping over the edge, but he was enjoying the moment and the love he still felt for the feline was as obvious as the nose on his face.

10

Two days later, a scribbled, handwritten note was delivered to Mickie's and Agatha brought it with her to Wilf's heavily guarded home, in the company of Percy, just before noon, the same day. My friend looked to have an extra spring in his step, as he opened the passenger door to let her out. I didn't know their sleeping arrangements, but I knew she was staying with him and to my well-trained eyes, they looked more like a couple, rather than two people who'd suffered a bad break up. What I couldn't tell from their body language, was whether this was a temporary arrangement. I wanted to pull him aside and tell him this was a mistake and he'd only get hurt again, but I knew I'd get no thanks for it. I had no option other than to let it play out. Paul had delivered Everton, Jimmy and me half an hour earlier and on the way over, I got that feeling again that we were being followed, although I saw nothing to back the hunch up.

We watched Percy and Aggie arrive through the long Georgian windows, in one of the rooms facing the front lawn. To say this room was a front parlour, was like saying the Royal Albert Hall was an intimate venue. Ginny stood next to me smoking and if looks could kill, the feline would have dropped dead on Wilf's sweeping driveway.

Wilf stood talking to Alec and Jim the mute, out of earshot and as I turned to signal to him that they'd arrived, the two men moved swiftly to the rear of the house, in something of a hurry.

The meeting was called by Wilf, so that we could all agree on the instructions Aggie was going to send back, in the hope we could control the next meeting and recover the missing piece. What I didn't know at the time, was that there'd been two messages waiting for Agatha at Mickie's, the other was a telegram, carefully folded and tucked into her shoes, along with three of the *Nine Lives*.

As Percy and Agatha strolled into the room, there was a commotion from the back of the house that took all of our attention. Alec and Jim, dragged in a ruddy faced visitor, who had not come willingly. I struggled to keep a straight face when I saw who it was. Before us stood nonother than my nosy nemesis, unable to wriggle out of Alec's grip, like a prize catch at the end of a line.

"I found him poking around in the boat shed."

Wilf's expression was sour.

"Let him stand on his own two feet."

"I told this goon of yours that I'm a policeman, but he didn't seem to believe me."

"Good evening Sergeant Fitzpatrick. I'd say you're a little out of your jurisdiction and perhaps even your depth. You'll forgive me therefore if I ask you what you're doing on my property?"

He straightened his clothing, while giving himself a moment to come up with a plausible reply and it was then he saw me.

"Him," was all he said, gesturing towards me.

"So, despite the fact that you smell like a brewery, you're telling me you've come here to question one of my guests?"

"He's a bum and up to no good. If I were you, I'd get this big bloke to throw him out."

Wilf rarely lost his temper, but I saw him clench his fists and sensed he was closer than he'd ever been to losing control in my presence and when he spoke again, it was through gritted teeth.

"Mr Prince is a guest and not only is he a close personal friend, but he is of great value to your country at this time. We both know there is no legitimate reason that could explain away your presence. Do I really need to call Percy Philips and ask him to clarify why you're standing in my home, lying to my face?"

Fitzpatrick's colour turned from pink to a deep crimson, but he said nothing else.

"I'll take that as a no and if my information is accurate, you can tell John Smith there was nothing to report Sergeant," he said, pausing to unclench his fists. He then turned his gaze to his two men, still standing beside the diminutive Irishman. "see to it he's given a lift back to the city. He's clearly in no state to drive."

Alec nodded, spun him around and followed him out the way he'd come.

Wilf helped himself to a stiff drink and lit up a smoke, as most of us opted for caffeine. Only Everton and Aggie joined him by asking for something stronger.

The seating had been arranged in an alcove so that we could sit together by the front window. Along with the coffee, we were tempted by a plate of what my father always referred to as *snorkers*. Namely sausage sandwiches. The pork, or lamb sausage, like most things during the war, was a sought-after commodity, so nobody needed to be asked twice and everyone tucked in. Most of us garnishing our sausage butties with brown sauce. Once satiated, everyone except me lit up and a much calmer and controlled Wilf, cleared his throat.

"I'd like to suggest we call the meeting at the marina, that way we can have extra bodies on the water if needed."

"It's a good place but they'll know you're involved if we do," Percy said.

"He's right Wilf, Albert Dock is near enough and if we meet after the shipping offices are closed, we won't be disturbed," I added.

"That'd work just as well and I can see to it that the dockside is deserted," Wilf added, then turned to Aggie, "will these people go for it?"

"I don't see why not," she replied.

Before we could discuss the proposal in any more detail, we heard the pop of a sidearm and Ginny went to the window and reported that one of Wilf's men was lying face down in a flowerbed. I got to my feet to take a look for myself and saw that the man's face was hidden in a bed of late blooming dahlias.

"Did you see the shooter?" I asked.

She shook her head and posed a question to all of us.

"Was anyone followed here?"

"I didn't see anyone but I got that feeling we were being watched."

"Just great Vic, keep it to yourself why don't you."

I didn't have time to complain. I wanted to say this was only a gut feeling and I saw nobody, but the truth is when I got that feeling it's never wrong.

Her piece was in her hand when she turned to face everyone.

"You armed Everton?"

“Sure am,” he said and despite all the nice words and discussions with my dad, I could see the bloodlust in his eyes.

“Follow me if you will, Wilf, you know what to do.”

“Please come with me everyone,” he said and they followed. I assumed he was leading them to what was once his cellar and was now his operations centre, that was bound to be the most secure place in the big old house. I was sorry I hadn’t brought my blackjack and quickly scanned the room for something I could use as a weapon. Then I saw it, a black, extremely ornate but well used poker. I lifted it and tested its weight. If I caught someone with this beauty, they weren’t getting up I thought and cautiously followed Ginny and Everton to wherever they were heading. Which was out into the large entrance hall, where I was just in time to see them cross the Italian marble, unsurprisingly taking a vertical path and vanishing though a small door, to the left of the main entrance, that I would have assumed was a storage cupboard. I followed with the hefty poker weighing down my gait on the right side. As I reached the door the popping sounds started up again.

Well-worn steps took me down to a dimly lit, musty smelling corridor, that veered off to the right and was lit by a line of bare, dusty, light bulbs, stretching away into the distance, that I guessed must be taking us under the driveway. I thought my light feet had concealed my presence, but when I heard Ginny call out to me, I remembered what she used to do for a living.

“If you’re coming Victor, pick up the pace.”

I quickened my stride and was soon at their heels, as the corridor abruptly ended and offered a turn to the left and the right.

Ginny pointed for me to follow Everton and she went off to the left, as an explosion of gunfire boomed overhead.

I followed Everton up another set of old stone steps, which brought us to another doorway. He pulled out his gun, licked his lips and put his free hand on the ancient doorknob and pulled the door towards us. I knew we'd both need to stoop to get through, but he hesitated, I assumed to get his bearings. From my vantage point it looked like the small door was hidden behind dense foliage, but the smell of gunpowder told us the shooting was close by. I leaned toward him and it was then I realised he was counting. He reached twenty and burst through the door leaving me in his wake. I followed him cautiously and saw him come up behind a stout man wearing an overcoat, who was hiding behind a tree and turned in surprise as Everton appeared at his back, smiling. The man raised his gun but Everton plugged him twice in the midriff in the blink of eye. I was still heading his way, when I saw movement to his right and knew I needed to act fast. I changed direction and saw Henry Jones creeping towards Cosgrove, staying low and making very little noise. He turned when he heard me coming for him, but I'd already primed my weapon and struck him with a hefty blow on the temple, that forced him to fall backwards and as I propelled myself through the dense wood and leaves all about us, Everton was clearly alerted. As Jones's head rocked back, from the blow I'd administered, he involuntarily discharged his weapon skyward and Everton fired once in his direction and I was glad I'd held my position. The slug might have flown over his head, if he'd remained in the crouched stance he was occupying before I'd lumbered into the clearing. My intervention meant that the bullet hit him plumb in the right eye socket and he was dead before his body hit the soft ground.

There was still shooting over to the right, where Ginny had exited. I followed Everton, who stepped over a dark-haired corpse, we assumed must have been Ginny's kill. We grew closer to the shooting and found Ginny and Alec, advancing and firing into an area that butted up to the edge of Wilf's property.

"We've got him cornered," she whispered.

"We will have if I go right and this big fella, goes left. I think they call that a pincer movement," Everton chirped in.

"Why I think you might be right sugar and there's something else, I don't suppose Mr Henry Smith knows about this place."

"Go on," I said.

"Now that'd be telling. It'll just be like cornering a mad dog back home. Follow and learn Victor honey."

She whispered something to Everton, they took up their positions and I stayed with Ginny. Our group edged forward with caution, firing randomly in the general direction of where they thought Smith was. It took a good ten minutes but felt more like an hour, until we heard an anguished cry. Ginny moved quickly, her gun still out in front of her. She held me back though, as we approached a sheer drop that must have been forty foot down. It seemed that Wilf had installed a deep ditch at the boundary of his property. We peered down at the crumpled corpse, that had once been Henry Smith, his eyes open in death, as if he couldn't quite believe the cruel twist of fate that had ended his existence.

*

Neither Ginny or Everton said a word on the short walk back to the house. Rather than retrace our steps, we took the more direct route to the front door, by departing the shrubbery and heading toward the curved driveway. We left Alec and Jim the mute to organise the grim work, that would involve disposing of four bodies. I've no idea where the cadavers were bound and frankly, I didn't care to know. We reached the house and Ginny pushed the door open and went inside. Everton was about to follow when I tugged at his jacket sleeve.

"What is it now?" he asked, his sullen expression as always matching his dead eyes, as they searched my face for an answer.

"Something isn't right."

"Did you hit your head during that ruckus Vic?"

I had a million smart responses, but this was no time for jokes.

"I've got that feeling again Everton. The same one I had the night Aggie's, Aunt's house, was bombed. Do me a favour, go around the back and find a way to get behind us?"

"Why?"

"Just humour me. If I'm wrong, then the joke's on me."

He held his hands up in mock surrender, then dropped them to check his gun, which he reloaded before edging around the side of the house and towards the boat house, where earlier, Fitzpatrick had been spotted.

I stepped inside the large entrance hall, the sound of my footsteps bouncing off the Italian marble and echoing around the large empty space. Elsewhere, the rest of house was quiet. Too quiet.

I pushed on towards the room we'd earlier occupied and even though my pulse was racing and my palms were sweating, I ignored my in-built alarm system and headed right for the source of the trouble. Before I did, I placed the poker on the floor. I hoped I was dead wrong, and they were all seated by the fire, drinking tea and eating cake.

Three figures stood by the fireplace alright but none of them looked happy. Percy was between them, his brow bathed in perspiration. What looked to be a Luger, was pointed at his temple and beside him, stood two skinny, white blokes, still wearing their hats. The thinner of the two removed his as I entered the room, revealing a thick mop of auburn hair. He had milk white skin and a strawberry birthmark on his chin and said nothing at first, but glared at me. I stopped fifteen feet from them. The gunman was a few shades darker but his eyes were a piercing blue, that didn't quite match his blue-black hair, or his complexion.

"We want dat girl," the man holding his hat said, spitting the words out in a thick, southern Irish brogue, "or he gets his right here and now."

"What girl?"

"Look don't play dumb wit me. You were at that house with her."

I smiled but I was sure my eyes didn't join in.

"Our friendly neighbourhood bombers no less."

I tried to lift the volume of my voice, hoping Everton would know something was wrong, as he was hopefully winding his way to our position.

"What are you waiting for? Go and get the bitch, unless you want to see your friend's brains splattered all over the nice wall coverings."

"Who are you?"

"None of your feckin' business."

"Have you come for the *Nine Lives?*", I asked, only looking for confirmation they weren't. Something told me these boys didn't even know what they were, and I was right.

"I don't what you're taking about. Stop wasting time. Go and bring her here now."

"I will, but first I want to know what this is about?"

"What's it to you?"

"Call me curious."

"I'd say nosy bastard. You're that private dick, aren't you?"

"That's right. Call it professional curiosity."

He looked across at the gunman who nodded.

"Hands on your head."

I did as he asked and he strolled over and patted me down, before backing up into the exact spot he'd earlier stood, a look of mild surprise on his face.

"I don't like guns. It wasn't a crime last time I looked it up," I added, still playing for time and simultaneously wondering where Everton was. I worried that any minute, Ginny, Wilf and the others would just blunder into what was unfolding.

"Look we'll do this and go. You'll never see us again. She and her boyfriend killed our brother back home. We caught up with her fella in some fleapit, up north somewhere."

"That was you?"

"Look stop wasting time."

"Even if you do kill her, you'll never leave this house alive. You don't know what you're getting yourselves mixed up in coming here."

"We don't care. This is a blood feud and we've sworn to carry it out, or die trying."

I heard something to my right. I couldn't identify the sound, but I would have bet everything I had on it being Everton. I heard another noise that I'd swear sounded like the rustle of clothing. I just hoped he wasn't planning on joining us in his birthday suit.

Before I could think of anything else to say. Ginny stumbled through the door to our right, a glass in her hand. Her eye makeup looking to have been deliberately smudged and she was wearing only one shoe. Her hair was in disarray and she'd unbuttoned her blouse almost to the navel, with only one button incorrectly aligned and fastened, protecting her modesty. She'd also pulled the blouse off her left shoulder, so that the strap of her bra was visible. It was an Oscar winning performance as she walked right up to the man holding the pistol, leaning forward, then grabbing hold of him, as though she was leaning down to pull off her other shoe. Both Irishmen were open mouthed. I've said it many times before. Ginny Merrill is an incredibly beautiful woman and they just fell for her act, hook line and sinker. By the time Everton had passed through another door that was buried in the wood panelling, on the rear wall, to my left, she'd pulled her pistol from the waistband of her skirt and between them, they'd turned the tables on our guests. Everton stood to their left and Ginny had knocked the dark-haired man's gun to the floor and I took her own weapon from her hand, as she fixed her clothing and Percy moved to my side.

"I didn't think you liked guns," the man with the auburn hair quipped.

"I'll make an exception this once, but if either of you think of rushing me, my colleague here will leave you bleeding out on the carpet, before you've taken a step."

They diverted their gaze to Everton, who saluted them both, his expression set, a customary matchstick protruding from one side of his face. They stood stock still.

We heard the others enter the room and a look of hate flowered on their faces at the sight of Agatha and I saw that she recognised them too. Wilf and the auburn-haired man locked eyes and again a flicker of recognition passed across the faces of both. Wilf was quick on the uptake and after a few short words with Ginny, he approached the spokesman and said,

"I'd like a word in private."

Ginny patted him down and nodded her head.

"Follow me please."

He did as asked, still fingering the brim of his hat as he went.

We offered his friend a drink and seated him on a straight-back chair, as we kept our guns on him. We all had a drink. It had been quite a morning. Only Everton remained standing, watching the other gunman like he was a lab rat. He in turn, glared at Agatha, as he sipped his Irish whisky and a frosty silence permeated the room, that I thought might not be possible to cut, even with a sharp knife.

Half an hour later the auburn-haired man appeared, still holding his hat. He shook Wilf's hand, gestured to his companion and the silhouette of Alec, accompanied by Jim the mute, appeared in the doorway. They escorted the two men who'd come to kill the Feline, out of the house.

I looked at him with an expression that attempted to convey numerous questions.

"They're IRA. We work with them."

"You're telling me the IRA work for the British Government?"

"Against a common enemy. It's a truce that's all. I reminded him of our arrangement and my contact over there spoke to him on the phone. The blood feud or whatever it is, is also suspended."

I smiled,

"Then I'll drink to truces all round."

*

We met at Albert Dock two nights later. It was a filthy night. Unrelenting rain beat down on us from above and the wind had picked up, but was much stronger on the banks of the river.

The meeting had been set for eight.

The windjammer was out on the Mersey, where I was told sat Alec, Jim the mute and Bill the skipper, nice and dry under cover, field glasses trained on our position. We thought we were well concealed by a seven-foot wall and the absence of any light during blackout. I wore a dark gaberdine mac, that was supposedly waterproof but even with my collar pulled up over my ears the rain had started to soak through. Only Jimmy Cohen who was to my left, wearing a waxed jacket looked reasonably dry, while Everton stood on the other side, in his own dripping wet overcoat, his back against the solid brick that housed a bank of three shipping offices. His expression was impenetrable, as the rain run off his hat like water flushed from a drainpipe. Percy and Aggie were huddled together out in the open, pretending to be the only two attending the meet. But they struggled to keep their sturdy umbrella upright, in what looked like a force ten gale.

By nine thirty, Wilf called it a night. He and Ginny were somewhere to our left, at a right angle to where Percy and Aggie waited. As we made the short walk back to the marina, it was agreed that somehow, they'd spotted that Agatha had company. As I mentioned, I thought we were well hidden, but Wilf explained that the German military had started to use something he called night vision goggles, enabling them to make out shapes in the dark. Therefore, he thought it was possible we could have been seen from a nearby vantage point in one of the many buildings, or warehouses in the vicinity. We agreed that when they made contact to re-arrange, we'd need to come up with a more robust plan of action.

We were all invited to the marina, which was members only and strictly reserved for the elite set. They were only influential because they had money. Most were involved in enterprises much more crooked than avoiding the occasional import duty, but they all had something Percy didn't. White faces. Little did they know that Wilf was inviting our melanin infused hides into their inner sanctum and if that wasn't bad enough, they would have choked on their *foie gras,* if they'd known a Jew was included in our party. Wilf had no issue bringing any of us through the front door, he'd proven that by inviting me to meet with him on many occasions, but in view of our clandestine arrangement, he thought it best to take us up to his private suite of rooms by another route. We made it to an entrance around to the rear but as Wilf inserted his key, the door opened, and Roderick Peters stood before us. We hurried inside out of the still driving rain to remove our sopping wet coats and a waiter took us though to a small sitting room, where a roaring fire had been lit. I hesitated as the others filed inside, spotting Roderick pull Wilf to one side. I noted that they spoke within earshot of Ginny. I hung back and saw him head upstairs, where I knew he kept an office. Roderick followed, a stern look on his face. Ginny walked in beside me and we headed straight to the drink's cabinet on the back wall, where she poured us both a good measure of brandy, as the rest of our group warmed themselves around the impressive fire, while making small talk.

"What's going on?" I asked.

Ginny's expression was impossible to read but her eyes showed concern.

"Jim showed up with a woman who claimed she was the courier, hoping to buy the *Nine Lives*."

I now understood the reason for the worry on their faces. Who was this woman? And if she was the genuine article, why had she changed the venue and why was Jim the mute with her? When I'd been told he was aboard *the Windjammer*?

"Are we being had?"

"I don't like any of it," she said taking a gulp of her brandy, drinking it like it was water, "if I didn't know any better sugar, I'd say they left us out in the rain to dull our senses."

"If you're right, what are they up to?"

Ginny turned to face the fire and was seemingly trying to bore holes into Agatha's broad back with her eyes.

"I wish I knew honey but one thing I am certain of, is that Miss Agatha is holding something back. I don't trust that bitch as far I could throw her, and I'd happily throw her carcass into the river, right this minute."

"Steady on Ginny, you're getting all Everton Cosgrove on me."

She ignored my quip and looked at her watch.

"Got an appointment?"

"Wilf asked me to go in after him in ten minutes, if he hasn't surfaced and bring Alec with me, if he turns up that is. Where the hell is, he?"

"I don't know but I don't like it. I've got a better idea."

"Go on?"

"Let me go up there unarmed and you and Everton follow, after about a minute. Wait outside for my signal. If I knock on the wall a couple of times come in hard and but if it's only the once, come in nice and easy."

"I don't know Vic."

"Let me get the lay of the land for you."

She was still staring at Aggie.

"I swear I'll shoot her in the head if he's harmed in any way and I find out she's behind this."

Her eyes filled with tears and I reached my hand out and rested it on her shoulder.

"That's unless Everton gets to her first."

She smiled through the tears and as Jimmy approached the drinks cabinet, I smiled in his direction and raised my glass, as Ginny turned her face away from him.

He put his thumb up and started to pour drinks.

I put my lips to Ginny's ear.

"We good to go?"

She nodded and I tugged at Everton's wet sleeve, indicating that he should follow me out of the room.

"We'll see if we can't rustle up something to eat," I said, lifting my voice over the roar of the fire, "I don't know about the rest of you, but I could eat a horse with a scabby head,"

We exited the room to a chorus of laughter and derision and once outside, I hurriedly explained our hastily put together plan. Everton nodded and reached for his gun and Ginny looked at her watch.

"That's ten minutes and no sign of him."

"He'll be okay," I said before climbing the stairs, praying I was right.

I'd met Wilf here half a dozen times before and knew the layout. The photos on the wall of the great and the good he knew personally. The fine wallpaper and its intricate blue pattern on a magnolia background, but it was all now a blur. I got to the top of the stairs and told myself to breathe. My suit and shirt still felt damp and I longed for a hot soak in front of my own fire, but I put that out of my mind and knocked. The door opened and as I crossed the threshold, I felt the cold steel of a gun barrel at my neck. I quickly captured the situation, frame by frame, my vision momentarily acting like the lens of a camera. I saw Wilf ashen faced, sat behind his desk. Somebody sprawled on the floor beyond the desk and as I was shepherded further into the room, I saw it was Roderick. Somebody had cracked him hard on the skull and knocked him out cold, but at least he was still breathing. Seated to the left of Wilf was a face I'd only seen once before. Miss Kaya Masondo, had been on the arm of a certain Everton Cosgrove at the White Oyster club when we'd met. She was holding a gun on Wilf and the killing machine looked comfortable in her hand. If she was a nurse my skin was white.

I craned my neck slightly to the left and my peripheral vision confirmed Jim the mute was holding a gun on me.

For some reason he was smiling. I'd never witnessed the corners of his mouth in an upward curve before and it was something I didn't care to see again, but it was Kaya who spoke,

"I want you to go downstairs and bring Agatha here and she can give us those pieces she's holding. Then you can accompany us to Percy's place and hand over the rest of them."

"Who do you represent?"

"Tut, tut, Victor, you don't really expect me to tell you that do you?" she said, then averted her gaze to Jim and said, "frisk him."

He did and I was clean.

"Good boy Victor," she said, then to Jim, "let the man breathe, he can hardly leave the room with a gun pressing into his windpipe."

He backed up and I turned as though to go but instead give the partition wall one good belt.

This brought the barrel of the gun close again, as Everton Cosgrove and Ginny Merrill strolled into the room, guns out in front of them.

Kaya reacted by climbing to her feet but kept her revolver trained on Wilf.

"Not what I was expecting," she said.

"Perhaps not sugar, but let me tell you that if you squeeze that trigger, you'll be in hell before your body hits the floor."

"That maybe, but I know what this man means to you."

Everton's face was more animated than I'd ever seen it.

"What's this all about Kaya?"

"Oh, come on lover, you've got eyes. It's exactly what it looks like. At least we'll always have Formby, Everton."

He laughed and I wanted to tell her that this wasn't exactly a good sign. He was hurt at being used, yet his dead eyes gave none of that away.

"Who are you?"

"My name is as you know it, it's just my purpose that I kept from."

There was movement behind us and in walked Agatha and Percy.

"We heard voices and thought you might need a hand with that food. What is this?" Percy asked.

"Meet Horatio Afia's half-sister," Agatha told us.

I'd never expected to see so many people crammed into Wilf's office and I was worried we might all be hit, if just a couple of the guns in play went off.

Agatha was smiling now and at first I thought she was looking at me but it was the beanpole of a man beside me.

"I thought I recognised you at the house but the smile gives it away. It's Jamie isn't it? Kaya's ex-husband? I've seen photographs of both of you. Your brother was so proud of you Kaya. He said you'd be running that hospital one day, but I don't think he'd approve of this."

Kaya looked angry, but this time it was Jamie who spoke and his accent was similar to hers. Was this the reason he'd hardly spoken?

"So, it's alright for you to steal from Horatio and make a score? But not for us?"

"Come on Jamie, how do you think Horatio happened to have them?"

"You don't know one damn thing about it," Jamie came back, his words rapid, his eyes on fire, "there were four of us guarding poor old Herbie, two on, two off."

"Whose idea was it to use the Veronal to kill O'Brien?" I asked.

He did a double take and peered at me as if he'd forgotten I was right in front of him.

"Her brother was the ideas man. It was supposed to be him and me, fifty-fifty, but after giving O'Brien a fatal dose of that stuff, he slipped me enough to send me to sleep. When the other two found Herbie dead and me snoring like a baby and those pieces gone, they went ape shit. They didn't trust a word I said after that, so I slipped away when we had a sudden visit from our superior officer. Then they tried to pin it on Horatio I heard and vowed to track him down, but the officer didn't swallow it, so they killed him right there and the rest you probably know."

"Let me guess the man they killed was Irish?"

"Do you read palms as well gumshoe?" he said, laughing.

"If I was reading yours, I'd say you have about five minutes to live."

The atmosphere immediately changed in the room.

I'd lit the blue touch paper.

“I think you’re forgetting who is holding a gun on who?”

“I think you’ll find it’s whom,” Ginny said and shot him in the throat. He put his hands up to his neck, followed by an anguished croaking sound I will never forget. He proceeded to drown in his own blood, fully aware his life was ending and that he couldn’t do one damn thing about it. The fractional hesitation from his concerned spouse was all Everton needed and he shot her twice, before she could even contemplate squeezing the trigger. The first killed her instantly through the heart, but like all good button men, Cosgrove sent the second to her head just to make sure. My suit was splattered with Jamie’s blood, but I was glad none of it was my own.

Ginny slapped her gun into my hand and went to Wilf, cradling his head to her bosom.

“Oh my god, oh my lord...” she repeated, overcome by emotion. I went to check on Roderick and shook him awake. He was fine but groggy, with a nasty bump on his head. Aggie was going through Kaya’s bag and a yelp of triumph passed her lips as she came up with one of the miniatures, that was allegedly required by her buyer to verify its authenticity.

Wilf kissed Ginny and stood, her hands still clinging to some part of him, so happy was she that he was still breathing.

“I say we leave this mess up here and retire to the fire downstairs. I don’t know about the rest of you but I need a stiff drink, also my clothes are still damp and I could do with warming my bones in front of that fire.”

*

Alec and Bill were waiting to speak to Wilf at the foot of the stairs. It seemed that Jamie had emptied their fuel over the side and made his escape in the outboard. They were eventually assisted by a crew from one of the working craft out on the river and towed into the marina by one of the pint-sized tugboats. Their reward was to go up to the office to clean up the mess we'd made.

We were back in the sitting room and I sidled up to Everton who was eying up the drinks tray.

"You okay?"

"Why wouldn't I be?"

"What happened to the man who wanted to get in touch with his feelings?"

"You see how far that got me?"

"Don't be too hard on yourself. You're not the first man to be duped by a good-looking woman and you won't be the last."

"I know it. Maybe you should have a word with your friend."

I turned to look at Percy, his arm draped around the feline.

"Sometimes you just have to let these things play out," I said, then patted his arm, "that was good shooting and no matter what you say to my face, it couldn't have been easy."

Ginny sneaked up on us and planted a kiss on Everton's cheek and squeezed his other arm.

"You saved him. I can never thank you enough Everton," she said, and her eyes were suddenly brimming with tears, "I lost my head up there and I could have got us all killed, what was I thinking?"

"You saw an opportunity and took it. There isn't a person in this room who wouldn't have done the same," I told her.

Then I poured the three of us a brandy and raised my glass,

"To Everton. A man I'm glad to have at my side."

"That goes for me too."

A brief and extremely rare smile momentarily appeared on Everton's face.

She then went off in search of her man, once she'd poured him a glass.

"Ginny's proof if you needed it, that there is somebody out there for you my friend. The Kayas' of this world you can count on one hand."

"Do you mean what you said?"

"Course I do, there's plenty more fish in the sea."

"Not that, calling me friend, I mean?"

It was my turn to smile.

I was never a fan of Everton joining Percy's outfit, but when I'm wrong I generally do it properly and I'd been dead wrong about him. He liked violence, there was no getting away from it, but I'd rarely met a more loyal individual and during this past year he'd proven himself on numerous occasions. I'd rather have him watching my back, than facing me in a gunfight.

I extended my hand.

"One hundred percent."

He shook it and I saw him grow in front of me.

"I'm honoured Victor."

Before we could seal our bromance good and proper, there was suddenly raised voices and we both turned.

Ginny was facing Aggie and her face was contorted with anger. It seemed that Wilf had quietly suggested that as there was now no buyer, she was free to accept Mr Churchill's generous offer, which he added, still stood, even if the previous offer appeared bogus.

"No dice Wilf."

"No dice? He puts his life on the line, opens his home and his business up to you, and all you can say is thanks but no thanks?"

"I didn't ask for any of this."

The room was suddenly as quiet as a mortuary. I signalled to Everton that we should perhaps join the discussion. He followed me over and as I flopped down in an armchair, he stood behind me and leant against the wall, popping a matchstick into his mouth. Neither of us spoke, but I saw a look on Percy's face that I recognised. It was a look of realisation. The penny had dropped into the slot. He looked at Agatha as if she carried some highly contagious disease and visibly shrank back from her.

"What it is baby?" she asked him, seeing the change in his expression.

"You've got all nine pieces, haven't you? That's why you stayed with me. Did you take them out of my safe when I was sleeping? I bet that was your plan all along."

"Percy don't act this way," she said, reaching for his hand, but he pulled it out of her grasp.

"Then hand me your shoes."

"Don't make me do this baby."

"Then hand them over, prove to me you're on the level."

It happened quickly.

She pulled her handgun on him and pushed it into his ribcage.

"Now stand very carefully Percy. We're leaving and if anybody gets any ideas about being cute, I'll clean his clock."

We all stood and watched her back out of the room, using him as a shield.

Everton tugged at my lapel and spoke quickly,

"I'm going after them. I'll make sure he's safe."

"Even if she buys it?"

"Just hold them in here as long as you can."

I let him leave, my heart pumping at breakneck speed again. It had been quite a night already. Ginny was the biggest problem. Even when I told her Everton had this one covered - not quite believing it myself, she still threatened to shoot me if I didn't step aside. I only moved when Wilf told me that the two Irishmen, who'd tried to kill Agatha a few days earlier, were currently his guests at the marina, awaiting transit back to the Emerald Isle.

All five of us dashed out into the still falling rain and saw three figures in the distance, down by the river. They were obscured by the drizzle and the lack of light. I also spotted the two Micks watching too, from the cover of a building to our left. Everton had caught them up and I held my breath as he went down on one knee. The pop of two shots was followed by Agatha going limp and falling to the ground. I was relieved to see that Percy was still upright. I broke into a run as Everton knelt over her body, no doubt to check if she was still breathing. Before I could get close enough to any one of them, he'd removed her shoes and rolled her body into the Mersey.

I stopped twelve feet from Percy and his face was impossible to read, as Everton led him away, still holding the stolen footwear.

I turned around and although I only glanced in their direction, I was sure the two men from Ireland were smiling.

*

The next day Wilf started pestering me. He wanted to know that all eight of the Nine Lives were in Percy's possession. I told him I'd find out, but I knew I couldn't face Percy right away. I didn't think it mattered that she'd threatened his life. She was gone for good and although she was no damn good, he'd always loved her.

I got up the courage after work on the third day. I asked Mei-Li if she'd walk over with me on her way to work. We ate a little earlier than usual, both bathed and changed our clothing and strolled across on a dry, cool, Autumn evening. We stood at the door, after I'd given it a rap and I was surprised when a grinning Percy opened up, but when I saw who was standing about ten paces behind him, my eyes couldn't quite square it with my brain.

His face fell when he saw my expression harden.

"I thought you were Paul, you'd best come in."

Mei-Li followed me inside.

"You're looking well for someone who died three nights ago," I said to the feline.

My girl ignored my frown and smiled at a woman she long called friend. They embraced as I fingered the brim of my hat and watched on, as in no time at all, both had tears in their eyes.

"I was sure you'd work it out Vic."

"Here's me thinking you'd be suicidal."

"If I had been, you didn't exactly rush over to comfort me."

That crack did it, I just couldn't prevent the corners of my mouth forming into something resembling a smile.

"That's more like it boy," he said, "come inside and let me make the world's greatest detective a drink."

I couldn't argue with any of it, some great sleuth I was. I'd swallowed the con; hook, line and sinker.

We all sat together and had one final drink, while we waited for Paul to fetch her father. It seemed that Percy had persuaded Agatha to let him finance her new life in Switzerland, where she and her father were bound that very night. He was giving them enough so that they could buy a place, that they eventually planned to run as a hotel. They both spoke of grand plans to stay in touch after the war, but I was unconvinced either one of them had the stomach for it. I just knew it was enough for Percy that she was still above ground. He told me that the Irish needed to think she'd died, because as far as he was concerned, they were never going to let it lie.

He explained that a couple of his trusted warehouse men, had a small vessel waiting to fish her body out of the drink, after Everton had rolled her into the fast-moving river.

"That water was freezing," Aggie piped up.

"It's a good job you agreed to wear my long johns under your clothes then," Percy added and we all laughed.

"Was Kaya's arrival at the marina part of the plan?"

"No way Vic, she played us good and proper. We owe Everton big time for his shooting and of course for his missing," Aggie added and that got another laugh.

"Where is the old psychopath?"

"It's his night off."

Paul eventually turned up, explaining that it was treacherous to try and drive without any lights and I had to admit he had a point.

Soon after, Mei-Li and I said our goodbyes and walked to the White Oyster club, still bemused and elated to know that Miss Agatha Hill, was still in the land of living.

Prologue

I sat in my office next morning after an early call from Wilf, assuring him that all eight pieces from the *Nine Lives* collection, were once more safely ensconced in Percy's safe. On my desk was a telegram, promising the earth to Agatha if she handed over all the pieces to a courier, who would meet her at an undisclosed destination overseas. We suspected whoever had sent the message was associated with German high command. I planned to hand it over to Wilf, so that his people could examine it and glean whatever information they could about the sender.

He asked me why she'd accepted Percy's offer rather than the promise of greater riches and I told him I didn't know. I hoped the answer was her love for my friend, but the cynic in me argued that she simply didn't trust the enemy coming through on their end of the bargain. At least this way she could make good on her promises to her father. I knew the payoff would have made a considerable dent in my friend's finances, but if I ever tried to discuss it with him, he'd start by telling me to mind my own business. If it got any further than that I'd expect him to say something like, 'its only money Vic and when people are dying like flies all over the world, you have to get your priorities right.'

I wouldn't have been able to offer an argument.

The ringing of my phone interrupted my musings and for some reason the chimes brought a sense of foreboding I can't explain. It caused me to pause and just stare at the black, bakelite instrument.

I eventually picked it up and said nothing. The same muffled, but definite female voice didn't wait for me to speak as always, and launched right into her diatribe,

"A visitor will wreak havoc on the eve of your wedding, but be patient with him Victor. He'll lead you to the final piece, as long as the low men of the city don't get to it first."

The line went suddenly dead. I knew enough to avoid asking questions, she was never going to answer. I still didn't know whose side my mystery woman was on, but I knew enough to keep the part about somebody spoiling Mei-Li's big day to myself.

..............................TO BE CONTINUED

COMING SOON: Vic Prince in King of the Jungle, Book Five in The Prince of the City series.

If you enjoyed this book, please be kind enough to leave a review and read on for details of all of the author’s other published works.

The Shifting

Doctor Stephen Forshaw belonged to one of London's oldest and wealthiest families. When he simply vanished into thin air, only to be followed one year later by his sons, Robert, Angus and Toby, no motive or clue to their disappearances was ever discovered by the police and their bodies were never found. Despite this, the authorities secretly believed that all four were dead and were certain that it was only a matter of time before their bodies were discovered.

Almost ten years to the day Stephen went missing, a boy matching Toby's description reappears at a disused farm in Hertfordshire. The boy has no memory of where he has been and doesn't even know his name, let alone why he hasn't aged one day in a decade. He is only aware that his life is in grave danger.

Reviews for The Shifting;

'**...**a penny dreadful mosaic... reminiscent of 19th century literary craftsmen...'

'A winning change from the usual magic and undead!'

'...totally engrossed by the twists and turns...'

Available in paperback and for Kindle;

Buy online at Amazon or order in at your local bookstore or library.

The Book of Souls

On the day eleven-year-old Imelda Stone discovers the reason she has always felt different from other children, her beloved father storms out of their home in the middle of the night. Days pass and when the police are called, a body is not located, nevertheless Edward Stone is presumed dead. But Imelda knows he is very much alive. One night, she hears a voice calling to her from the old, dry well at the bottom of the garden and all her hopes and fears are realised at once.

An enemy older than time has waited to unleash his master plan. His intention is to kill his old foe Edward Stone and wreak havoc on Earth, but he hasn't counted on a gifted eleven-year-old standing in his way. In a breath taking series of events, Imelda seeks out her missing father, faces up to a ruthless killer and in a pulsating finale enters an alien world to rescue her fatally wounded father and save the human race from certain destruction.

Reviews for The Book of Souls;

'Record breaking event! My son read 'The Book of Souls' in less than 24hrs!'

'…. It's a little Alice Through the Looking Glass meets Harry #Potter meets Lord of The Rings…'

'.... A tale to delight the imagination...'

Available in paperback and for Kindle;

Buy online at Amazon or order in at your local bookstore or library

Lost Boys

Renowned criminologist Delbert Walsh has spent five long years searching for his only son during the political upheaval of 1970's Liverpool. Walsh believes boys have been disappearing from the area for over twenty years, but the lack of a single clue has driven the retired policeman to flirt with alcoholism.

Carol Blake and her three male friends find their lives in danger when they become acquainted with Walsh, as the net closes in on the perpetrator.

Reviews for Lost Boys;

'...atmospheric, creepy at times and on the edge of your seat stuff...'

'...Mackenzie Brown creates a community of people who stand up from the page. They live and breathe.'

'...Brilliantly told...'

'...the conclusion to the book hits hard. It's a story that will stay with me for a long time...'

Annie's War

This is the true story of ordinary people living through extraordinary times.

Annie Newland's life starts in 1914, in the worst of circumstances, but this is only the beginning - as life continues to put obstacles in the way of her happiness. *Annie's War* is an epic tale of family drama and a love story set between two world wars.

This is the uplifting and fascinating true story of the early lives of the author's grandparents.

Reviews for Annie's War;

'**...**An ordinary Liverpool family which lived through extraordinary times**...**'

'...brilliant and so moving ...'

'This is a great read, especially for anyone who loves family history.'

'...a marvellous story and a great read...'

Available in paperback and for Kindle;

Buy online at Amazon or order in at your local bookstore or library

Prince of The City: The Cat's Whiskers

In this first instalment, Vic Prince is on the lookout for a missing Persian blue cat everyone seems to want, while also searching for the missing son of a beautiful widow who unwittingly puts him on the trail of a hired killer.

As if that isn't enough, his best friend is wanted by the Russians, who are on the trail of a cache of missing guns... but what has this all got to do with bodies found floating in the river, with no identifiable cause of death?

Reviews for POTC: The Cat's Whiskers;

'The book is a marvel...'
'…unique and intriguing…'
'...depth, colour and intrigue...'
'Great pace, great characters and an intriguing plot line…'

Available in paperback and for Kindle;
Buy online at Amazon or order in at your local bookstore or library

Prince of The City:
Nine Lives

In book 2, Vic is engaged by the wife of a wealthy business man, Cyril Longthorn, who believes her husband is being held against his will by a criminals' who are stealing from him.

He is forced to travel to the popular seaside town of Southport, to unravel the mystery, but gets far more than he bargained for, when associates of Cyril's are murdered before he can talk to them…

Reviews for POTC: Picture Purrfect;

' Pulp fiction at its best - marvellous….'
'…. A great follow-up to The Cat's Whiskers….'

Available in paperback and for Kindle;
Buy online at Amazon or order in at your local bookstore or library

Prince of The City:
Picture Purrfect

In the third instalment, Vic is engaged by Henry Swan, Hollywood's biggest black film star; who is in Liverpool to promote his latest movie. Swan has a rather delicate problem and needs all of Vic's unique skills to track down blackmailers, who are hoping to extort three pieces of the 'Nine Lives' from him. If that isn't difficult enough, a mysterious female killer is on the trail of the three pieces and is aided and abetted by a hard man from the North East, who makes Everton Cosgrove look like a choir boy. In a rip-roaring finale, Prince risks his own life to help Swan and keep the curios out of enemy hands.

Reviews for POTC: Picture Purrfect;

'Vic is back better than ever….'
'…. quite simply the best book in the series so far….'

Available in paperback and for Kindle;
Buy online at Amazon or order in at your local bookstore or library

Ten Little Thrills

Ten Little Thrills explores the thriller genre with ten diverse stories from the pen of Mackenzie Brown.

Fans of Brown's noir influenced Prince of the City series will be pleased to find Vic Prince solving one of his earliest cases and from Brown's third novel Lost Boys, the brilliant Delbert Walsh attempts to catch a cold blooded killer on the fog soaked streets of 1950s London.

Eight further stories will either set your pulse racing, or bring you out in a cold sweat, but for those who prefer to use their little grey cells, there is even a classic whodunnit set in Venice during the 1950s.

Ten Little Thrills is the perfect read for every fan of crime fiction.

Reviews for Ten Little Thrills;

'The suspense was palpable ….'

'…. I was sweating right along with the main character and hope to never be in a similar situation! Enjoy this book!'

Available in paperback and for Kindle;

Buy online at Amazon or order in at your local bookstore or library

About the Author

Mackenzie Brown was born and raised in Liverpool, UK, where he lives with his wife, two daughters and pet cat. With 9 published novels already under his belt, Brown is planning to write another book in 'The Prince of The City' series of hardboiled detective stories set in 1940s Liverpool. Brown's inspiration for writing was borne out of wartime stories shared with him by his grandfather and personal hero, Angus Mackenzie Brown, a character featured in the book 'Annie's War'.

You can connect with Mackenzie Brown at the following locations;

His website - mackbrown.weebly.com/index.html

Twitter - @ScribblerBlue

Facebook - www.facebook.com/MackBrownBooks

His blog - mackenzie-brown.tumblr.com/

LinkedIn - www.linkedin.com/pub/mackenzie-brown/48/579/72b

Goodreads Book Club - www.goodreads.com/author/show/6434456.Mackenzie_Brown

Pinterest - www.pinterest.com/mackbrownbooks/

Printed in Poland
by Amazon Fulfillment
Poland Sp. z o.o., Wrocław

65955375R00108